GRAND GESTURE

REMEMBER THE RUIN, BOOK 3

A. R. SHAW

APOCALYPTIC VENTURES

For Bainbridge, my respite

By gnawing through a dike, even a rat may drown a nation.

— EDMUND BURKE

FORWARD - ANGUS

Damp mist settled against his navy polyester suit sleeves and lay upon the backs of his hands like a gossamer veil. Angus MacPhie found this annoyingly like Scotland. But despite that, he stepped into the crowd and immediately assessed the situation. If there was anything he knew about ferry lines, it was how to get to the front of one. One must weave between the gaps, no restraint held for decorum. No pushing or shoving, mind you, but brushing by skirted the edges.

It didn't take long for a native Scotsman to figure out a puzzle. When he first took the job and moved to Seattle with his wife Jacqui, they'd refused to live in the warzone of downtown. It was a shame what had happened to the Emerald City in the past decade at the hands of a city council bent on a social experiment gone so wrong most businesses had packed up and left long ago, leaving boarded-up storefronts on every block in their wake. Addicts ruled. Not only did they buy and sell drugs openly, but they also used them as well. Criminals had rights and all victims were just in the wrong place at the wrong time or were more likely, in their view, the villains themselves. Because they worked for a living and therefore aided in the evils of capitalism. Or at least, that's the roundabout logic Angus perceived from the situation. Which made him a target a few times a week because instead of living in Seattle, Angus and his wife lived on nearby Bainbridge Island.

When they'd to move to the Seattle area and refused to live in a downtown skyrise, that left little choice but to find a way to commute from somewhere farther out. Like many do, Angus joined the ranks of those living beyond the insanity within a reasonable commute zone and instead found a nice little house on the island only a short ferry ride away. Close enough to commute and yet too close to the madness.

Bainbridge Island commuters used the Washington State Ferry system. And since Angus lived within walking distance of the ferry dock, he didn't even need the use of his car and avoided paying the exorbitant fees associated with parking or riding his vehicle onto the ferry. If only he'd been the only one to think of this convenience in an increasingly overcrowded situation...it seemed many had the same idea as the numbers increased by the day. Even after the not-too-distant ferry attacks. He wasn't on board the day the ferries were bombed and sank to the bottom of the Puget Sound, along with the passengers who lost their lives at the bottom of the sound that day. Some of them he knew or had known, at least, by the arrangement of their faces. He'd been home with an early video call that day and it was only after he heard the sirens and alarms from somewhere in town that he walked down Winslow Way to see for himself what all the commotion was about.

A month later and with armed escort, ferries were back in order. He was lying if he didn't admit he hesitated a bit walking the plank from the pier. But just for a second. Business must go on; bills needed paying.

Instead Angus followed the crowd of daily commuters, doing his best not to step on the heels of the ladies in front of him. How they walked up those steep, wet Seattle streets in two-inch stilts confounded him. It wasn't practical. Could not be comfortable. And perhaps they didn't move nearly as fast as he wanted them to go, either. Being a Scotsman, Angus didn't much like the feeling of walking through a funnel like a herd of sheep. Shepherding was a trade he'd tried to avoid as a boy and wasn't about to volunteer for the sheep's position now. But here he was on his tenth year already and twice a day he made the trip from Bainbridge Island to Seattle and back again. Always joining the herd.

Except that instead of following along, Angus had learned to weave. He wouldn't call it pushing. That wasn't what he did. There was empty space at times. He never made contact with anyone. He simply led by example and maneuvered through the gaps at a quick pace. It was the only thing that made sense if you thought about it, and Angus was a sensible man. He had to get to work on time and dallying behind mocha-carrying, impractical shoes-wearing commuters didn't quantify his goal of docking, walking two blocks, catching an elevator up twenty-three stories and logging into his meeting at precisely 8 a.m.—on time.

He wasn't sure what the rest of the daily commuters' schedules, or lacks thereof, were but that was his ritual. And he was going to make it to work on time if it killed them. Or at least, in his mind, that's what he imagined as he held onto the chrome pole while the ferry neared the monoliths on the other side of the waves.

But they were at least ten and a half minutes away yet. So the window drew his gaze. It was a middling bright morning. There would be rain by the end of the day, he thought. No surprise there. Just a wee bit of sunshine peeking out in a ray behind a cloud. A few gulls screamed past the bow of the ferry in hopes a human might offer up a torn end of a croissant and when they spotted the flaky flesh, their wings would bank and swirl around as if they were feeding from the gods below them.

But Angus diverted his attention from this ballet playing out again and instead he caught sight of a patron's laptop streaming the news in a seat nearby. It was that Gowdy guy, and Cameron Hughes again. He could see there was a heated discussion and if memory served there was a restraining order between the two there for a while. But he couldn't hear a word because the guy holding the laptop was jabbering with the lady next to him.

"What are they up to now?"

"I swear, Senator Mathus can't leave well enough alone."

"What? I'd want to know. Think about it. No more unsolved crimes. You do the crime, there's no more denying it. That's it. Swab positive and you go to jail. No more wasted trials. Do you know how much that money that is?"

"Do you know how much it's going to cost us? I mean, there go *all* our rights. Think about the health insurance. My mother had Parkinson's, for instance. You don't think they're not going to find that in my DNA and raise my health insurance rates? Or deny me coverage altogether. Heck, they might even start sterilizing people or keep them from reproducing based on their DNA simply because a grandmother had early onset dementia or breast cancer or heck...what if she was nearsighted?" She gasped on purpose. "And come to think of it...I'm not so sure my little brother and I have the same father. There was a time when our parents took a break and mom was a bit friendly with the milkman...and since we're in our forties, that's a whole other can of worms I think needs to stay in the closet."

The man holding the laptop had his mouth open after that, staring at her like he wasn't sure what to say next. He finally closed his jaw. "You've got to be kidding me. It'll never come to that. They won't expose all of that information."

Her hand flung to the computer screen. "What do you think they're talking about? No holds barred. They're going to let it all fly, open domain."

Angus had enough of their version of the news and interrupted, "Can you turn it up there? What is it that they're saying?"

Angus wasn't sure if the lady next to him was his wife or a colleague, but in any case, the man holding the laptop seemed almost delighted for the interruption and nodded quickly, "Oh sure," he said, and then Angus noticed other heads nearby bobbing closer to hear the news. He felt a little embarrassed by his own intrusion but was glad he took the initiative in the end. Perhaps he even saved an argument?

"...a gross intrusion of privacy," Gowdy said, with his hands splayed out like an offering. "I mean this is the most fundamental rights violation I can think of. A person is born into this world with a certain amount of basic rights but the minute he or she comes forth out of the womb, you're going to a swab and own...*own them*," he said, with conviction. "That person's physical makeup? I'm still trying to understand how in the hell you guys pushed through the Kinder Euthanasia Bill, extending the Afterbirth Abortions to age *five*. I'd like to know what in the hell your definition of murder is, anyway. Just because one parent decides to give up their rights, they can petition to have the child from their union...killed?"

"Euthanized," Cameron corrected. "It's a humane practice in the Netherlands, and why should an unwanted child be brought in this world when the lives of the parents are affected negatively? They have rights, too. And the world is overpopulated as it is. Hopefully soon, they'll extend the option to orphan homes, relieving states of the tremendous burden of debt incurred to raise an unwanted child."

"Because the child in question is a living, walking, and talking human being. Because they have a beating heart and are fundamentally *alive*. At five years old, they can think and make decisions. They can feel pain, remorse, and love," Gowdy said in a hoarse whisper, with his palms facing up.

Cameron shook his head and smiled as if he were talking to a student. "It's done very peacefully," Cameron said softly. "They're unaware of anything. They're entirely dependent on a set of parents where one or both of them are unwilling or unable to care for him or her. What kind of life is that? We're saving them from a lifelong struggle."

The guy with the laptop said, "He seems pretty calm so far." He grinned up at Angus.

Angus blinked and couldn't help widening his eyes. He swallowed hard but smiled back quickly to deflect any discussion.

"He's probably under court order," someone else said.

On the screen, Gowdy looked up. "You just said it yourself. *Life*...you're taking his life. That bill was only meant for those with a terminal illness, but we're talking about perfectly formed human beings now."

"You can look at it that way," Cameron Hughes said. He was leaning back in his chair, almost relaxed, except Angus noted the man had his right leg crossed over his left knee at the ankle and his ankle was systematically tapping thin air.

"He shouldn't relax. Gowdy's about to spring," the woman said.

Cameron's right arm came out and his finger pointed at Gowdy. "But think of all the innovation, the medical triumphs..."

"Phts," Gowdy said, and flayed his arms out and laughed. "Yeah," he said and rolled his eyes. "The medical triumphs. You sick f..." he buried his forehead between his hands and made a moaning noise.

"Oh no," laptop guy said in almost a whisper. "Here it comes..."

"Shh..." someone said.

Angus noticed every head leaned a little closer to the screen.

And then all of a sudden, there was a tremendous jolt.

1

DANE

Dane read the words she'd texted to Matthew and then stuffed the phone in her sodden jeans. It was stupid for her to reach out and text Matthew for help but for once, Dane wasn't sure what to do next. The palms of her hands were cut up and bloodied, but the rain had washed away the worst of it. She smeared the rest on the sodden ground as she dragged herself from where the blast catapulted her into the air and landed her hard to the ground, and then she realized she was too exposed. The dark figures of people rushed by her in a grassy field, screaming, running. Not one of them stopped to see if she was all right. So she found refuge behind a utility building.

It was suddenly dark as night. It was daylight before, wasn't it, when the blast happened just before? She wasn't sure but was now wondering if she'd been knocked unconscious there for a time, because it was raining in sheets. Sirens were drowned out by alarms and the amber glows of fires were everywhere in the distance.

She'd been running through a park. Right? That's what happ...and Bill. That wasn't a dream. She'd ended him. She remembered that now. The blood. She looked back at her hands again. No, she'd washed his away in a sink. In a park sink. She was still in that park. That's right. So...the blood on her hands now was her own. And her ankle...that's why she couldn't walk. It wasn't just sprained. Something in there was no longer functioning. That was a big problem.

The worst problem was getting to the ferry dock. She had to get back to Bainbridge Island. To Matthew's borrowed truck. It was just a few miles but now...now, something had gone wrong. There was an explosion. A bad one. There would be more security...if that were possible. But that would take time. She needed to move. She needed to hurry and at least get in line. Claim she lost everything in the chaos. That would work. They couldn't detain everyone, right? She at least needed to get closer to see the situation.

Pulling her good leg up as close as she could, Dane pushed her hands against the rough building, pushing herself up and bearing her weight on her right leg.

"The pack?" she said, scanning the ground. Other than the golden light of distant fires...it did little to aid her view of the park grounds. She hopped around the corner and held onto the building to peer further and then saw the bathroom facility building where a motion detector light was affixed to an eve. Just beyond the door, there was a body on the ground. A woman with dark hair.

Dane flashed on the lady in the bathroom from earlier, the one she tried to hide bloody sink water from. She was young. Maybe early thirties. A brief smile. Or no...she didn't even look at her. But she was alive then. And now she was dead. Just like that.

Dane let out a breath. And despite the high-pitched alarms, intermittent screams, dogs barking...her eyes stuck to the stranger's body before her. In the rain.

She wasn't sure what was wrong with her. Here she was

feeling remorse over a stranger's tragic death and yet only hours before she'd killed someone outright. *I mean...he deserved it*, she thought.

Then she blinked and realized her gray pack lay only ten feet to the right of the body. She hopped away from the eve of the building and into the downpour as she took a tentative step. A blinding flash of pain shot up her leg and into her hip and she reached for the ground or lose balance all together.

"Crap! I can't...fall." Sucking in several deep breaths, Dane pushed herself back up on her right leg and hopped, eyes on the pack, and then hopped again. She kept her left leg up and out of the way, arms ready to catch herself if she stumbled. A few more unsteady steps and then something dark coming in fast from the right ran right into her.

ANGUS

"What the hell happened?" Angus yelled, sliding his wireframed glasses up the bridge of his nose as he stood, still holding onto the back of the plastic chair vacated by the guy with the laptop as the boat weaved one way and then to the next. The laptop itself was lying on the blue carpeted floor. The blank screen had somehow dislodged from its keyboard. That was a damn shame, Angus thought. He looked around for the owner of the broken laptop. He had that woman with him. The one he wasn't sure if she was the wife or a coworker. But they were nowhere in sight. The other commuters, however, were running everywhere and the whole boat kept dipping dangerously from one side to the next, and that's when Angus shook his head and then shook it again, and then stuck his finger in one ear...and then the piercing ringing took over, instead of what he didn't realize before was the unnatural sound of nothingness.

Then guys with the blue uniforms showed up on deck. Some were pushing people back through the double doors as waves breached the railings, leading them in by the arm back inside... where he still held onto the chair to stay level.

Their eyes...all of them, were wide open in terror. And that's when Angus let go of the chair and walked forward from the cabin. He grabbed onto walls and went out onto the deck and looked beyond the commuters. Then he looked up at the monoliths in the distance. The Emerald City, the one he saw everyday...it was golden now, in spots. With black plumes. Thick smoke and fire engulfed the very buildings before him.

"Mother of God!" he said, and a passenger brushed hard past him, hitting his shoulder and knocking his glasses straight to the gray-painted deck. Of all things, somewhere in Angus's mind he wished he'd invested in that Lasik surgery now more than ever, but he just never found the time to take off work. He dropped to his knees and brushed his hands around the rough floor as a wave splashed over the railing, turning the light gray deck to dark gray in an instant. Running footfalls landed between his arms, in front of his hands. A shoe shoved something small and metallic that skittered a foot away against the half-wall railing and Angus leapt for that space in the void. His hand grasped the metal frames, fingers pushed where the lenses should be and found they were still intact. He flipped over with his back against the wall and looked up again at the burning city as he looped the wire frames around his ears and saw again...the gold and the black.

"Well, at least we'll turn around. We'll head back to Bainbridge," he said to no one in particular.

Then the captain's voice came over the loudspeaker. And though people were screaming, he still caught the words, "... State Policy, that in case of catastrophic events, the ferries return to the Seattle dock."

"What? That's rubbish. The boat's nearly full." He turned to see another passenger standing nearby. A lanky guy who seemed to have a perpetual smile for as long as he had known him. He didn't have a name as far as Angus knew. He just rode the ferry on the same schedule with him each and every day for years.

The guy lifted his hands, smiled even wider despite their circumstances and shrugged his shoulders, like, *What are you gonna do?*

Angus turned away, gripped the railing with both hands, and shook his head. Of all people to be stuck with as they neared the burning city...the happy guy.

3

MATTHEW

They'd landed, finally, and were on a bus with flashing lights and sirens, along with every emergency vehicle available, heading into the fireball of a city as the highway next to them looked like a string of lights, six lanes deep, desperately trying to get out, but only inching along at a snail's pace.

Matthew had given orders to his crew as they sat patiently but with an eerie silence between them while they drove like mad into the blaze.

Owen sat next to Rebecca in the bench seat, her head leaned against the windowpane so that her red curls bobbed up and down with the rhythm of the ride.

Matthew met eyes with Owen in the dim light as Owen chewed on his fingernail, staring up at him, and then leaned over closer and whispered, "What are you going to do, Matt? I know she texted you. I know what you're thinking."

Matthew wondered what the answer to that question was, himself. The truth was, he had no freaking clue what his own intentions were. He had no idea what condition Dane was in or what kind of help she needed. He'd texted her back but so far there was no reply. *Games?* he thought. No. They'd been through too much together for that and hell, Dane didn't play games. That was the old girlfriend, he reminded himself. The one that died because of him.

"I don't know, man," Matthew said with a slow shake of his head. "I'm going to do my job."

Owen's eyes bored deeper still. "I know that much about you, Matty...but then what? This..." Owen looked around. "This crap's not going to stop. Everyone's got an axe to grind and if it's not one group it's another. Just promise me this." He scrunched in closer to Matthew. "If you decide to bail...let me know. I want to know." Owen glanced at Rebecca and then back at Matthew and nodded. "We...want to know."

Matthew ran his teeth over his bottom lip before he answered. But he didn't really answer, he just returned a sharp nod of his own.

It wasn't as if the thought hadn't crossed his mind a thousand times since he and Dane separated, and the entire world went to hell even more than it had before. When did that happen? What pinnacle had he crossed? It'd been a gradual thing. And somehow, losing Tuck was the line in the sand. The thing that made him teeter. Things had been increasingly more nuts but Tuck's death in Chicago...for some reason, that was it. The bottom just dropped out after a while of doing his job and seeing for himself how fucked up it all was. Tuck didn't even die due to the collapse of society. He died sacrificing his life so that Dane might have a fighting chance to live. That's the thing that stuck with him. That's what mattered. That's what he couldn't get off his mind. That man died for humanity. He had integrity. He'd died with it intact when the world had long lost the definition of the word.

"Promise me, Matt," Owen said again. "I want to hear you say the words. I want to know you're not going to just disappear on us."

Matthew blinked slowly. "I promise."

4

DANE

"Hey, hey, wake up. We need the bed."

Dane's eyes flashed open. Bright, bright lights. And worse yet, someone was wailing nearby. The sounds made her shudder. Make that more than one person. But it was the smell that clued her in. She was in a hospital, or at least the hallway of a hospital.

"Look, I know it's rough. Can you call someone to come get you? We need the bed," he said again. "Your bill's already been paid so you're free to go," the man said as he checked an iPad.

Dane shielded her eyes from the bright fluorescents above. And then suddenly everything went dark.

"It's all right people," the man yelled. "The generator will kick on in just a second. Stop screaming!" he yelled really loud. "Remain calm, dammit!" He pulled Dane up by the shoulder. And then, in a more measured voice, he said, "Look, I'm sorry, but we need the bed. Here." He pushed something into her hand.

She blinked her eyes, adjusting to the dark and in the now-darkened hallway, emergency lights flickered on and then she realized what she didn't before—the hallway was moving. "So dizzy."

"Steady yourself then. The exit's that way," the nurse or whatever he was, said, but she had no idea which way he was pointing. "Here. Take the crutch. Your ankle's swollen and you likely tore something, but we can't do x-rays at the moment. You also have a laceration on your head. Again, your pupils are fine so it's not likely a concussion, but you did lose consciousness. The man who brought you in felt bad—said he plowed right into you. He carried you here all the way from the park. In short...it's not that bad, and we need the bed. So hey, it doesn't matter if you're ready or not, you've got to go. Make your way to the exit and call someone to pick you up or catch the next bus out of town because it's getting crazy here. Oh and, please check in with your doctor as soon as you can for follow-up care. And you might want to take an anti-inflammatory."

She leaned on the crutch because he was already wheeling the bed away and then remembered her phone. Slapping a hand against her thigh, she felt the hard rectangle still in her pants pocket.

The orderly's voice yelled, "Get out of the way, people," as he pushed the bed deeper into the dark cave of the hospital corridor.

"Wait," Dane said. "Where's the exit again?"

He stopped and turned around and pointed again, "That way. Just follow the glow."

5

ANGUS

"**. . . M**ust *remain seated,*" they announced over the loudspeaker.

Angus only caught the last bit, yet when he looked around, no one was seated. Instead they wandered aimlessly at sharp right angles in attempts to get a view of the tragedy unfolding outside, trying to get a signal on their failing phones or trying to edge away from the looming danger. The panic subsided in angry wafts like a lightning storm on its way to farther fields as each outburst diminished, and Angus returned to the cabin since the guys in yellow vests were now herding the stunned ones away from gawking at the smoke-filled Seattle skyline.

He stopped one of them with a straight arm to the chest. The man only looked down at the arm preventing his advance. His autonomous movements proved he too was out of it.

"Can you tell us what we're waiting for? If you're not going to return passengers to the island where we live, and you're not going to dock, are we just going to stay floating here until we run out of fuel and every man has to pick up a bloody oar? Is that it?

That's not a sensible plan." He had not meant to spawn rage toward the end, but he did. And didn't give a damn if spit flew.

The crewman didn't respond. He just continued to walk right on by, ushering another passenger inside the cabin like a zombie.

He didn't have any answers. That's what Angus came to. No one had answers. No one was in charge. This was all a bloody mess.

Angus turned his attention back to the burning city. But with all the racket of the sirens blaring, he heard the familiar engines rumble and soon the ferry was gurgling again in the water, not away from the flame...toward the flame.

A squawk over the loudspeaker and then, "...picking up passengers. Remain calm."

"Remain calm?" Angus said to himself and a woman inside the cabin shrieked and then promptly fainted, her body landing hard on the old linoleum flooring. No one seemed concerned.

"Mother of God..." Angus said, shaking his head.

And why wouldn't she scream? The skyline was filled with thick black smoke billowing into the sky even more than before. And when he looked again, fresh red flames were spewing from the tops of the Columbia tower and when he looked closer still, there was debris falling from the windows. It only took him a split second to realize what he was seeing wasn't debris but for now that's what he would tell himself. The streets must be littered by now. They were headed into hell...the exact opposite direction anyone wanted to go. But he supposed if they were going to pick up survivors, that was a good thing. What a mess...

"Maybe shepherding wasn't such a bad career choice after all."

6

MATTHEW

On 3rd Avenue, in front of a pyramid-topped building over fifty floors high, their bus finally stopped even though debris dropped from the smoke-filled sky. Teams spilled from the bus and ran to the equipment truck amongst orders yelled from hoarse throats, barely discernible over wailing alarms and the rushing sounds of blazing fires.

The orders weren't necessary. As if on autopilot, Matthew's team knew what they had to do. The terrified fled the towering marble building, tearing eyes wide just as Matthew and company headed into the blaze with ventilators on. Their small crew of eight ran into the marble-lined foyer and suddenly stopped. Emergency lights flickered and reflected over the shining marble floor.

"...twelfth floor," came the garbled voice over his mic.

"Repeat?" Owen said.

"Survivors on twelfth," Matthew said.

Lee pulled the universal elevator key from his vest and slid it into the lock on the chrome panel to the left of the door.

"Shafts clear!" Owen shouted after peeking above through the dark crevice above for any sign of fire.

"Check the cars for survivors when they reach the lobby, but stand back," Matthew called out, and they spread out to ensure each car was empty, though when the doors opened, heavy smoke spilled out.

"Twelfth floor, huh?" Matthew said as they piled in. "Hit tenth, Rebecca."

"Let's make sure the peekaboo feature works first," Lee said as he stepped into the car. He inserted the elevator key into the panel inside the elevator, held the 1 button and then released it quickly. The closed doors opened briefly and then shut again quickly. "We're good to go," he said, stepping out again.

"Great, let's wait a second for the others to catch up. They've got the high rise packs."

Matthew nodded and was thankful that Lee remembered his elevator certification training. Now was not the time to skip tests when it mattered most; though his team didn't often find themselves fighting fires within walls, their lives depended on it. He also realized he needed to get his head in the game. Missing these things, even though he was used to fighting fires in the woods, could costs lives and that's not what he was there for.

As they waited for the rest of the crew to catch up, they heard lobby music over their respirators. A few heads turned to the others.

Owen said, "How can that be possible? Should have shut off by now."

"Name that tune," Lee said, amused, going along with it anyway.

A few heads bobbed, then Rebecca shouted excitedly, "That's 'How Strong my Love Is' by Otis Redding," with her fingers pointed into the air.

They all laughed at her.

And then silence fell as they watched soot-covered, disheveled workers scurry out of the stairwell, running wildly for the doors behind them. Matthew glanced at Lee and saw the transformation he knew was coming. With that one look they remembered. They remembered why they were there and swallowed. Grim faces replaced the smiles while they waited for the next car to take them into the flames.

"Where the hell are the packs?" Owen said.

"That's a lot of hose they're hauling," Lee said. "Might take a while. They were parked a few buses back."

"Well, there's not going to be much left if they don't hurry," Owen said as he shot a penlight beam into the hoist way again, checking for fire.

Then they all stood there, and Matthew realized they were staring at him.

It was Chicago all over again. That's what they were saying without an uttered word. Only this time, which one of them would it be?

"No way, Matty," Owen said suddenly.

Matt wasn't sure what he meant but then...something caught Matthew's eye to the side.

Before he could respond, there was a commotion behind them in the building's convenience store where they sold quick afternoon snacks and things no one really needed to busy people in three-piece suits. There was someone in there. Why hadn't they left with the others? There was another man in there too. The first guy...the clerk with dark hair nodded his head, his right hand raised above his head. He took a step back.

A slight tickling shiver, a soft salute of hair across the nape of Matthew's neck. "Get down!" Matthew yelled at the top of his lungs.

Owen tore Rebecca to the floor as everyone slammed to the marble before the explosion ripped through the store clerk's chest, sending blood spraying to the wall behind him, and a shot echoed off the stone walls.

Already on the run, Matthew didn't even think. He scrambled over the others, grabbing his axe by the very end of the handle.

Time slowed as the gun turned on them and Matthew's eyes met pools of hate. He sent the axe flipping through the air, end over end, landing with a hard thud in the gunman's chest as if it were a tree trunk.

But the gunman wasn't down. He didn't even drop the gun.

Matthew's eyes met his again as he raised the handgun up into their general area.

But Owen was watching too...and before Matthew could move, Owen sped past him and made it half the distance before there was another flash of fire from the muzzle, and this time Rebecca screamed, "No!"

7

DANE

A shining diamond pierced her sight down the narrow, dark hall. The horizon slid around in waves. With her squinted eyes, Dane made for the wall to brace herself but the moment she put weight on her ankle, white lightning pain shot up through her knee and somehow right into the back of her butt.

"Mother fuc..." Dane said, gritting her teeth, and instead of stabbing herself each time she tried to take a step, she ended up using the crutch, sliding her left leg and then, eventually, after what seemed like an hour, limping out the doorway. No matter how dim the light, it was too bright.

Dane wiped away a fine sheen of sweat across her forehead and looked out into the scene of chaos before her. She squeezed her eyes shut and then opened them again. For a second, they focused, and she watched people run from one place to the next. Cars and emergency vehicles blocked the road and adjoining intersection. But what really caught her attention was the smoke and fires in the distance, then the horizon began to tilt. "What...?" Pressing her eyes closed again, Dane leaned against the brick doorjamb and felt her side pocket for her phone. She'd called him, hadn't she? Not really called, but she'd texted him. She remembered that much. Where could he be? Did he even know where she was? She hoped he remembered he could track her.

She opened her eyes again. Just breathe. Focus on the screen.

On my way, it said. He *was* coming. She hadn't imagined it. Then the words fuzzed out and Dane shook her head as her eyes filled with tears. Why had she asked for help? The blood she'd spilled, the explosion, the man knocking her to the ground. Chaos all around her. Dane pushed her injured leg out before her and slid against the wall down to the ground as her tears spilled.

She looked down at the message again as people rushed by, yelling, screaming, cars honking, explosions in the distance, yet close enough for Dane to brace herself against the door. She flipped past the message from Matthew and to her pictures within a closed folder. She rarely went there. Her memory was good enough. Now was the time to remind herself why she was on this journey. She wasn't really vengeful. She didn't want to kill anyone. She took no pleasure in the act. What she was doing had a purpose. And one photo reminded her she was human in an inhuman world. She swallowed, held the image close and whispered, "I will do anything to protect you."

8

ANGUS

As the ferry docked, Angus gawked at the commotion below on the car deck as he leaned too far over the railing. Engines started at the head of the pack and roared like agitated bubbles below a tight cork. Lights flashed and horns echoed against the steel.

"No! I'm not getting off! Are you kidding me?" a driver said and shoved the ferry officer out of his personal space.

"Sir, get in your car and disembark now," he said, pointing to the exit.

"No. You can't make me. Take the car. I don't care. I'm not going in there. Are you insane? Look at it, or did you not see the fireballs dropping from the sky as we approached? There's nowhere to go, man...I'm not leaving," he ended in a reasoned tone.

The guy next to Angus said, "I thought we were picking people up. Not getting off. That's what they said, right?"

"Move!" boomed another voice.

Angus shrugged. How was he supposed to know? Heck, they were pissing in the wind as far as he was concerned.

That's when he heard the metal gangplank slam down with a crashing bang, causing even Angus to flinch.

"Everyone off," yelled an officer with his rifle in one hand and a megaphone in the other.

"You can't make us disembark. We can refuse," came the voice of the passenger who had lent his computer screen earlier.

The officer stared at the skinny man and slowly swung the business end of the rifle in his general direction.

The man eye's widened and he looked at his female coworker. "Can you believe this?" he said.

It wasn't a rhetorical question, Angus realized. He actually wanted her to answer, as if he was stuck in a dream and didn't know it.

"Bullocks," Angus said under his breath as passengers shuffled toward the exit. He was slightly hoping there would be a resistance, a fight—there were more of them than there were crew. They could take them, couldn't they? But then Angus also knew history and human nature. They would shuffle in line while the few ordered them around.

That's when Angus thought of Jacqui and ran a hand through his thinning hair. She would have charged at the man with the gun. Led the revolution. She was going to be pissed. The only sight worse than an angry Scottish man was an angry Scottish woman. His eyes widened at the thought and he turned his sight to the right, thinking if he could only steal a boat he could get back to the island. His eyes scanned to the right, and that's when he saw it.

9

MATTHEW

"Well, it didn't take you long to make that decision," Owen said as he lay on a well-manicured rectangle of grass outside the building, with Rebecca rummaging through their meds.

"Shut up, you're bleeding," Rebecca yelled as she wrapped his arm with gauze and glared at Matthew.

Owen stretched out his good arm. "My *mouth* still works..." Owen said, protesting. "It went right through. It's not that bad, babe. Same damn arm as before, though."

But because of the look Rebecca beamed at him, Matthew said, "What? Why are you mad at *me*?"

Rebecca pulled the tape from her mouth, tearing off a piece. "Did you have to miss?"

With his hands up, he protested, "I only had an axe, Rebecca." He shook his head. "I...look, we'll finish this job and then I've got to find her. Rebecca, you stay with Owen. I'll finish this with the others."

"I don't know, Matty. This isn't going to end well. Look around. You sure you wanna go in there?"

And he was right, Matthew thought. Sirens competed with

shouting and gunfire merely blocks away. It was like something out of a World War II movie, only it was happening all around them, in real time.

"I think you should just give the others the option to leave, too," Owen said.

"That's desertion. You realize that?" Matthew said. "That's what we're doing."

It was Rebecca who said it. "No. Desertion is when you give up on a full army and go home."

"No. Desertion is when you forsake a cause you gave an oath to. That's what we're doing. We were all standing there that first day with Tuck, remember that? No matter what you do, don't lie to yourself. It's desertion. That's the fact," Matthew said and returned Rebecca's menacing stare like some Mexican stand-off. He wanted to make sure they understood they were taking on the stigma of having abandoned their honor, disgracing their oath, as he was about to do.

"You're both wrong," Owen said finally as he lay on the ground between them. "We're not forsaking or giving up on anything Tuck taught us. We're trading causes. We're joining Dane's war. This one's fucked. They're doing it wrong. We can't continue being the clean-up crew after the fact. We have to fight back. You can't tell me Tuck would turn down that chance." He raised his arms and pulled his injured arm out of Rebecca's grasp. "This is only going to get worse. No one's doing anything about it."

"Ooh!" Rebecca said, her eyes bright. "We could be like those vigilante fighters and stop the terrorists. Just the four of us. Covert-like."

Matthew shook his head. They were just proving his point. "You both scare me," he said. "I think the world has enough of those at the moment. Look around. Let's just get through this and find Dane and then decide our next step."

"Stay right here...unless shit starts landing near you." Matthew flipped his respirator in place and hurried through the smoke back into the burning building.

"We'll just wait right here..." Owen called after him. "Coming up with world-saving schemes and stuff while our hero puts out the fire."

Matthew smiled as he walked inside and met up with the remaining crew again, trading concerned looks with the others. "He's okay. That was a close one, though," he assured them.

The elevator doors dinged, and one set of emergency workers walked out, giving instructions to the others entering the car, while Matthew checked his watch. He wasn't sure when the notice came in but there it was: a Dane Talbot message glowing in green on the tiny screen. But it would have to wait because as he stepped into the elevator, he was also stepping into a Faraday cage and there were no messages in or out that way. It gave him a mental moment to think things through. It gave him a moment to change his mind because if he was going to change his mind this was his last chance. He was pulling others into this now. Was it the right thing to do? Was he going to get them killed like he did his ex-girlfriend? It wasn't just him and Dane fighting her personal war and more than that, he had to be certain he was the kind of man who could see it through.

The elevator doors closed.

"Matthew," Lee said, "they told us there're transients up there who've climbed the stairs up to the twelfth floor. We're told not to engage them."

"How can you say that? They're shoving people out the opened windows," another fireman said.

That was all Matthew needed to hear.

"Listen up," Matthew said. His voice boomed over the increasing chatter. So much for a mental break, "Axes out. If anyone *engages* with you, *engage* back. Defend yourself. We're not here to play Mad Max with the deranged. We're here to pull out any survivors and to mitigate fire damage where possible."

Matthew looked at the lights on the elevator and as the others took out their axes, he realized he'd left his in the dead guy in the lobby. "Crap," he said.

"Here," Lee said, handing one to him. "I had an extra."

Matthew wrapped his hand around the handle and thought, *Lee...he can handle this without me. He's a born leader.* And then the next nagging phrase...*Yeah, but, no one can handle this alone.* He'd proven that.

Then the elevator doors opened.

10

DANE

"Ma'am…miss?" came a voice in an Indian accent.

Someone nudged her knee. Immediately, Dane braced her arms in front of her face, fists clenched at the same time. Her phone went sprawling on the concrete walkway before her.

She watched through slitted eyes as a dark arm reached for her phone.

"Don't touch it!" Dane seethed.

His hand withdrew, and she scrambled for the phone.

"I meant no harm, miss. I'm your driver. You sent for me. I was told to pick you up here." Then he hesitated and checked his phone for something. "You are Dane Talbot, correct?"

She didn't know what to say. Did Matthew send a car to pick her up? That would mean he couldn't get to her or he wasn't coming at all. He must have tracked her location. "Yes, I'm Dane Talbot," she said and curiously, she wasn't sure why she felt disappointed all of a sudden.

"That was nice of him." She had to admit, she was having a hard time functioning.

And then in very quick English, Dane could barely keep up

with, the driver shielded her and started yelling, "Get back! Watch out! Can't you see she injured?" as several emergency workers rushed past and shoved her into the metal frame as she tried to stand.

"Come on," the driver said, and she let him help her get to her feet. "Here's your crutch. Let's get you out of here. These people. They're craziness," the driver said.

"Wait. Did Matthew Brogen send you?"

"Take another step, that's it; lean your weight on me. The vehicle's right over this way—you see it there? We'll have to hurry," he said in rapid-fire English.

She looped one arm around his neck and used her other to brace against the crutch.

And he was right, there was another firetruck coming their way but there was no way the truck was getting through the roadblock in the intersection.

Dane looked in the distance but couldn't make out which vehicle he referred to, and her eyes were still having trouble focusing on anything for too long without having to blink hard and tight. "Wait, how did you get through this mess?"

"I have my ways, ma'am. My name's Nehale, by the way."

"How did you say that?"

"Like knee and hall," he said.

"Ne-hale, who sent you?" She tried it out for size and asked, but before he could answer, a spray of gunfire erupted not twenty feet away as a man sent bullets into a nearby car with the passengers inside. Dane automatically dove down behind another vehicle, but Nehale did not. She looked up from her position and watched as he stood tall and pulled his own handgun from somewhere, took a perfect modified Weaver's stance and fired back with a dead stare.

Stunned, she demanded, "Who *are* you?"

He reached for her and waved his fingers a few times. "Come on," he said without taking his eyes off the scene before him.

She didn't move.

"I said, come on," he said, flashing angry eyes at her and back.

Dane reached for her crutch and noticed her hand was vibrating. She swallowed hard and grabbed the crutch. She could whack him with it, but something told her that wasn't a good idea.

"Who the hell are you?" Dane said slowly.

He took his attention off the danger ahead and reached down and pulled her up. "Right now, I'm your driver, Miss Talbot."

11

ANGUS

Down the gangplank...Angus shuffled along with the rest of the herd, their footfalls slamming against metal, the entire pedestrian crossover creaking with their weight. What if something fell on them? It would wipe out entire sections, killing them all.

Don't think like that, he thought and looked out the side gate as the traffic slowed up ahead. Someone shouted, "Keep going!"

What if someone else had the same idea? But so far, no one neared the independent fast ferry boats and they were hidden from view of the dock in their overhang from the boardwalk. It would be a race, he knew this. They were the size of a small yacht, only faster. He couldn't be the only one to think of them. He'd have to jump the herd and then find his way down the plank, cut over to the next pier and climb a few gates, bypassing the security guards without anyone knowing...and then...and then...he wasn't sure what came next, but it was worth a try, wasn't it? He was a criminal now, he thought. He'd already crossed that line, just by thinking what he was about to do...but then he looked again at the city before him as he came to the opening at the end of the tunnel...and yes, he was a criminal in the making now. A smile spread over his stubbly Scottish mug. "Och, aye."

12

MATTHEW

Listening carefully to the cadence of his respirator, Matthew couldn't help but think this was Chicago all over again. He gripped his axe handle more tightly. It was what he expected but also the worst he could imagine. The same scene. Tall building, everything ablaze and nowhere to go but a fast way down. His only reprieve was knowing Dane wasn't in there with them. He'd give anything for a forest fire...at least you could run and escape or die trying. But the walls...way above the concrete ground, Tuck fell to his death. The thought made him swallow despite the lack of saliva in his mouth.

Stop, he said to himself and just like every time before, he stepped off. "Let's go," he ordered the others and pictured Dane, the image in his mind where she lay in bed as he was sort of planking over her body, caught in a trance. Her long dark hair sprawled out over the white pillowcase like a starfish. Her red lips were swollen from the brush of his whiskers. A rare look of need and vulnerability was upon her face. Just for him, there were no walls there, just for a moment.

He cleared his throat, and wiped this image, too, from his mind. Born again into the fire, Matthew led into the blaze.

"Watch out!" Matthew yelled a few steps later, as an image ran by, causing him to take a step back. At first, he couldn't understand what his eyes were telling him. The man's tall, emaciated body was bereft of a shred of clothing, and barefoot.

He ran past them from left to right like a scared rabbit. All helmets turned, tracking the movement through the fiery hallway, and for the briefest second, Matthew thought it was funny, but before he could turn his head left again, because he knew in the back of his mind, he knew it was a distraction; something was coming...and then it happened before he could stop it.

A slam to the side of his face shield briefly sent starbursts through his vision, but then Matthew turned to face his assailant.

"Axes up!" he yelled and wished the moron standing before him holding the end of a lamp had hit him just a little harder because now he was going to hurt him, badly, and he was just a strung-out kid really, only in his early 20s.

"You should have tried harder," he said.

Lee yelled, "Watch it," and then everything happened at once. Several more locals came out of nowhere, all threatening to use whatever heavy object they could find in an office.

Instead of fighting the raging fire, they were suddenly in a gang battle with drug addicts.

"This is our floor! You're trespassing" yelled the kid, his eyes bulging from whatever drug was rushing through his veins. Once Matthew wrapped his gloved hand around his throat, he shook him a little until he dropped the lamppost and then shoved him into the elevator.

Lee had a hold on another strung-out individual, not much different from the first, and did the same signaling to the rest of the crew to deposit their assailants into the same hot elevator box while one fireman held the nozzle end of the hose pointed in their direction.

One kid stepped forward with obvious burns to his legs and hands.

"Don't do it," Matthew said. "One spray from Billy at this distance and that's 400 psi to your chest. Trust me, you'll wish you'd been shot instead."

"You can't do this!" the kid screamed. "This place is ours!"

Matthew shook his head at the insanity and then Lee inserted the silver elevator key into the left slot and pressed the first-floor button and stood guard to make sure none of them slipped out before the doors closed.

Matthew radioed ahead, "Five meth heads, coming your way. Police assist, or social services needed." He shook his head, knowing they needed more than a social worker for this bunch.

"Sure they can't stop the elevator on the way down?" a fire-fighter asked.

"Yeah," Matthew said, "Lee plugged the code for ground floor special delivery. Nothing they do will open the doors. They should have taught you that," Matthew said, looking at him suspiciously.

The rookie shrugged and then redirected the hose to what it was intended for.

Matthew watched him walk away and noted his form. Then he looked at the others stacked up against an encroaching flame. Their positioning. How they interacted. They weren't prepared for this. Among the crew, it was only Lee shouting orders that he knew was fully trained. "This is suicide," Matthew said to himself as he joined the firefight.

13

DANE

"I thought you said *driver*," Dane said, balancing on one foot staring at a BMW motorcycle that resembled a large gnarly wasp. Nehale quickly straddled the machine and motioned for her to get on behind him.

Without answering, he took her crutch and tossed it to the ground and said, "Put this on. Keep your head down," handing her a helmet.

"Where's yours?" she said, taking it and slipping it over her head.

"That is mine. Don't lose it," he said, and before she could say anything else, he started the engine, looked around and began weaving through traffic at a professional pace. She had to hold onto his thin middle with a tight grip. He'd done this kind of thing before, she decided. A man didn't drive through jammed traffic like this without a lot of experience. But who the hell was he? The lingering question kept her guarded against him, yet she had to hold on to the stranger or risk falling off. If Matthew didn't send him, who did?

"Hold on," Nehale said, leaning one way and then another. She leaned with him, as he weaved from one opening to the next at a high rate of speed, but she suddenly felt like she was going to lose what she didn't have in her stomach and had to close her eyes. He couldn't hear her so there was no sense in trying to ask him questions then. Then their speed increased dramatically, causing Dane to hold tighter to his leather jacket as they hit the open road on Highway 5. Dane looked around him after a while, seeing they were headed to the heart of Seattle. "Where are you taking me?" she asked.

But he either didn't hear her or he wasn't going to answer the question, leaving her no choice but to hold on and continue to swallow the rising bile in her throat.

After speeding past several more stalled and parked cars in an increasingly congested area, Nehale finally resorted to the pedestrian sidewalk and traversed the thirty-foot slope downhill, causing Dane to slide into his back.

At a slower pace, Dane asked again, and again he did not answer her.

That's when Dane began contemplating the rate at which she could dive off a speeding motorcycle and the survivability factor when he finally slowed. When she looked up, she recognized the ferry terminal pedestrian gate.

Her hands were clenched and still shook as if they were still riding as she took off the helmet.

"Don't go to the hospitals," Nehale said.

Without explaining she'd been unconscious when she arrived at the hospital, she said, "Why?"

"If you have any problems at all, text me. My number is in your phone now."

She shook her head and swallowed. "Who are you? Who sent you?"

His deep dark eyes darted to the guard in front of the ferry terminal and he nodded to the guy.

"Wait. What did you just say to him?"

"Don't enter that gate; go to the one on the left. He will let you in. Wait for Matthew there. He'll be here soon."

"I want answers, Nehale," she said as she hopped on one foot, keeping her weight from her other ankle as the guard approached them.

Ignoring her, he said, "Here," and pulled a backpack from his saddle bag.

Stunned, she slipped her arm through the sling.

"Keep this with you. There's extra ammo and a full magazine inside, along with food and medical supplies. Again, text me with anything you might need."

"Seriously, who are you?"

He smiled and nodded. "Those are answers you already know," he said and slipped the helmet over his head and sped away.

She watched him pick up speed and zoom farther down the road. "What the hell was that?"

She hadn't expected an answer but a deep voice behind her said, "Come with me," in a raised voice. When she looked up, the officer had his baton out and raised. He grabbed her with a tight grip around the left elbow and though her initial response was to protest, she realized he was actually holding her up off her injured leg and helping her to the gate to the left, just as Nehale indicated.

Flashing on the image of the mysterious man standing in the middle of the road firing back, she wondered how much a *Nehale* cost? A hell of a lot more than Matthew could afford. And then the answers came to her in a rush...she just didn't understand how.

"He's supposed to be dead," she whispered.

14

ANGUS

When was the last time he'd climbed a fence? *How hard could it be?* Angus thought as he stared at the eight-foot chain-link and then turned in an inconspicuous half circle to see if anyone watched him. One guard had his back turned to him, staring at a man and woman on a motorcycle that just pulled up to the curb. Angus slung his briefcase over the top of the fencing where it landed with a drowned-out thud. Then he grabbed the fencing and looked back to see the officer approaching the woman as the motorcycle sped away. *Great,* he thought. His focus was on her. Clenching the wire, Angus stuck the toe of his leather dress shoe into an opening and then grabbed onto the gate with his other hand and stared at the top, immediately realizing this was going to be harder than he first thought as the wire dug into his hands. As he struggled to take the next step, he felt a whack on the back of his leg and quickly let go, falling to the ground after gaining nearly two feet.

"Did you lose something?" the officer said in an even tone.

That was the first thing that made Angus stand a little taller. He didn't answer right away because the officer, still holding onto the woman from before, looked around Angus to see his briefcase on the other side of the locked gate. And then nodded at Angus.

"This is your lucky day, my friend."

Angus tilted his head to the side a bit and then stared at the woman, who was notably calm.

Something's not right here.

"What's your name?" the officer asked.

"Angus McAlpine."

"Angus, are you headed back to the island? Was that your intention?"

He paused. "Yes, officer. That was my intention."

"So you know how to operate that boat right over there?"

Angus turned his head and noted a speedboat moored right next to the fast ferry. It was smaller and likely faster. "I do," Angus said, standing taller still.

The officer nodded and handed Dane's arm over to Angus.

"Um, okay," the officer said. "You're to take her with you and make sure she gets to her vehicle. Is that understood, Angus?"

"Yes, of course."

"If I find out you didn't do as asked, I'll..."

But Angus didn't let him finish. "I will make sure she gets to her vehicle, sir."

The officer nodded as he unlocked the gate and looked around as he did before to see if anyone was watching them.

"Go on," the officer said with a sharp jerk of his head. "Get out of here quickly and avoid the Coast Guard at all costs."

Angus put the woman's arm around his shoulder and helped her hobble through but before the officer could close the gate again, he said, "Angus...if you're caught, you don't know me. We never met. Understood?"

Angus nodded his head.

The woman didn't say a word.

15

MATTHEW

"Did he make it? Is he coming?" Owen asked for the millionth time as Rebecca stood up in front of their spot on the ground, shielding her eyes from the smoke. "I can't see. There's a few coming out," she shouted.

"We need a truck," Owen said, looking around.

"Where are we going to find one around here?" Rebecca said as another siren screamed by.

"I don't know, but we can't stay here much longer," Owen said as he braced his arm against a wave of pain.

Rebecca had just turned to see him double over. "You need pain meds."

"No," Owen said. "I can't take that again. Not now. Come here. Help me up. We need to get him out of there."

"You're still bleeding," Rebecca said seeing a red bloom on the bandage she'd wrapped around him.

"Can't be helped," he assured her.

"We should get you to the hospital," Rebecca said.

He shook his head, looking at her with a smile. "No, darling. No hospitals. What once was will never be again. What we need to do is get Matthew, find Dane and get the hell out of here."

She nodded and looked again to the smoke-filled building. "Look," she jumped up and down. "There's Lee. Lee's coming."

"Okay. Okay," Owen said, holding his arm again since she'd bumped his wound unintentionally.

"Lee!" Rebecca yelled with her hands acting as a megaphone. "Lee!" she yelled again and then waved her hand above her head, so he could see her.

"Great, but where's Matty?" Owen said.

"I don't know. Lee will know. He doesn't look upset so Matthew's fine. Probably," she said.

"There he is," spotting Matthew coming through the doorway dragging a gurney with a body along behind him.

Lee yelled for paramedics and soon Matthew handed the gurney over to a few EMS workers.

"Is he going to be okay?" Rebecca asked Lee.

"Yeah...dumb kid lost oxygen."

"Matthew all right?" Owen asked.

Lee chuckled, seeing Matthew walk their way. "Psh, Matt's always all right."

Owen nodded as a smile spread over his face as he approached.

"You two done resting? Ready to go?" Matthew asked them.

"You?" Owen asked, knowing Lee would ask the next question.

"Going where?" Lee said. "Where are you going?"

Matthew nodded and turned to Lee and wiped the smeared sweat from his forehead. This wasn't going to be easy. "Lee, you're a good man. And now you're in charge of these imbeciles. Don't let them get you killed," he said and patted Lee on the shoulder.

Silent. Stunned. "You're leaving? You're all...leaving?" Lee said.

"Yes. We have a few things to do. You have my number if you need any serious help," Matthew said and began to walk away.

"Wait. What? What am I supposed to do? What do I tell them?" Lee asked.

Matthew shook his head. "I don't really care. Just don't let them get you in a tight spot." He turned and walked on.

"You're all going? You can't do this, Matt!" Lee yelled, stopping Matthew in his tracks.

He turned around.

"You guys, you're just deserting your post?" Lee said in a disgusted tone.

"Lee, there's a time to be faithful to a cause and then there's a time to see the writing on the wall. Look around you. They do this for fun, man." He shook his head. "We saved that kid in there and he had no business in that position. He could have got us all killed. They're playing games with all of us. Enough." Matthew pointed beyond him and realized he was yelling the words and spitting at the same time. "Look around you, man. This isn't a cause. This is chaos. This stopped being honorable a long time ago. There's nothing to save here, don't you see? They *want* it this way."

Matthew's words were never truer, as suddenly another building merely two blocks away exploded with what they knew was yet another bomb set by someone with a grudge, causing the four of them to crouch to the pavement.

"I'm coming with you, then," Lee said.

"We've got to get out of here," Owen said, coughing, "or we'll get blocked in."

Running east, Matthew checked the first truck they came to.

"Are we stealing vehicles now?" Rebecca said.

"Borrowing," Matthew said. "We're borrowing vehicles." Though the door was locked.

"Hey! Stop!" someone yelled behind them.

"Oh crap," Lee said.

"Matthew Brogen!"

In his mind, Matthew flashed on that day so long ago in front of Tuck. It was the way he said his name, only this time, there was a slight Indian accent as he said the words. Matt's hands lifted away from the vehicle he was trying to break into.

Owen shot him a warning look from across the hood of the truck.

Matthew turned around, hands in the air.

In front of him stood a tall skinny guy, not what he'd imagined, with dark skin and dark hair so long that it edged the shoulders of his black leather jacket. He was straddled over a parked motorcycle leaning to one side. Curiously, he wasn't a cop. Matthew dropped his hands.

"Who the hell are you? And how do you know my name?"

Instead of answering the guy reached into his leather jacket.

"Hey man," Matthew said, thinking he was pulling a gun.

"It's all right," the guy said slowly, pulling a black rectangle from his jacket and tossing it through the air for Matthew to catch.

"What? What is this?

But before the man answered he set something else sailing through the smoky air.

Matthew scrambled to catch the small black object as well. "What's this for?"

Without saying a word the guy had already pulled a black helmet over his head and grabbed the handlebars, lifted a knee and sped away past them with his black shield facing them.

"What the hell was that?" Owen said after a moment. "What just happened?"

"What did he toss you?" Lee said more specifically.

"A phone and a key fob," Matthew said, palming one in each hand.

Rebecca bounced. "Press the key fob."

Matthew raised his eyebrows and thumbed the rubber button.

16

DANE

They stood there on the dock staring at the boat sloshing in the water.

"You don't know how to drive a boat, do you?"

"No," Angus said, without hesitation.

"You said your name was Angus?"

"Yes."

"All right then. Help me in the boat, Angus. We'll learn together."

As he stepped over the side, they heard another explosion too close to their location and then people were running and shouting close to the gate they just walked through. He stared at her warily then.

"What?" she said, holding the gun out in front of her. "It's a reflex. I'm not going to shoot you if that's what you think." Then she added, "Yet."

"Can you point the damn thing at something else, then?" Angus said and reached for her unarmed arm to brace her weight as she crossed over the ledge and into the boat. "A busted ankle?" he said looking down.

"Yes," she said but then they both froze momentarily as shots were fired nearby again.

"It's the gate lock. They're coming. Quick, start the engine," Angus told her.

"I don't know how to drive it, either," Dane said.

He looked around quickly. "Well, you point the gun. I'll figure this out. I thought there'd be a cord to pull or something. Ah, a key..."

Dane heard him mumbling while she kept her eye on the gate area and hobbled her way to the seat next to him.

"It's not that hard, really...just like any engine," he said, when she heard the boat rumble and come to life.

"Will you just hurry? Go, go!" Dane yelled and steadied her aim at the dock.

Angus found the shift. "It's like a car really," he said as he pushed a lever to reverse and looked behind him.

"Hurry, they're coming," Dane said and slid up her position, pressing her back against the seat a little higher and gripping up on the stock, aiming. Then she had a thought. "If I run out ammo, he said there's another loaded magazine in my pack."

"The officer? Nice of him. Who was that guy?"

Dane didn't know what to say. She didn't really know Angus either and thought the less he knew the better—for both her safety and his. And her silence was just fine because as people rounded the corner, she closed one eye and squeezed the trigger, hitting a metal beam but sending an unmistakable message at the same time.

Heads bobbed around the corner. Then the muzzle of a weapon.

She found it ironic—for a no weapons zone, there were plenty of them now.

Angus arced the boat sharply away from the dock and sped away as Dane watched as the people came into the clearing and spotted them, their boat, and then focused on the larger boat in front of them. It was like watching a swarm of feral dogs go for the last hotdog on earth, one person climbing over another. Dane turned away when the guy with the gun pointed at the guy next to him. She heard a shot fired behind her but didn't look back. At the gate, they were fast friends but now they were enemies. How fast humans turn on one another.

"Hold on," Angus said and as he turned harder still, he picked up speed, sending her farther into the seat. With the immediate danger gone, she slid down. Then she gripped the seat. "Wait. Not so fast. Easy..."

"...getting used to it," Angus yelled.

"Do you know where we're going?" Dane yelled, suddenly worried.

"Yes," he said, delayed. His hair streamed back like the wings of Mercury, and she wasn't so sure he knew his way back to the island. It was one thing to be a passenger for years and yet another to be driving.

He must have sensed her conclusion when he glanced at her and said, "I've ridden the ferry for years. I know where we're going."

"Okay," she nodded. She'd take that answer for now and hoped so, because they weren't going back to the inferno behind them.

17

MATTHEW

B*eep, beep!* came the noise of a polished black SUV with bright headlights flashing.

"No way," Lee said.

"Do it again," Rebecca said.

"Who was that guy? Why would he just give us...maybe it's stolen?" Owen said.

Matthew closed his fist over the key fob and poked at the phone. "It's not stolen," Matthew said after he scrolled through a bright screen.

"What do you mean?" Lee said.

Matthew let out a breath, then pocketed the phone. "Come on," he said in a dark tone. "Everyone in." Then he stopped in his tracks and looked each of them in the eye. "But listen...this is the demarcation line. Remember that. From this point on, we're no longer servants."

"You say that like it's a bad thing," Lee said.

Matthew would have bet Lee was the one to argue for staying. "It is, isn't it?"

Lee shook his head. "That all depends on the one you're serving."

Owen raised an eyebrow. "See?"

That saddened Matthew. "All right. Come on."

"Where we going?" Rebecca asked.

"To pick up Dane," Matthew said.

"You say that like it's so normal," Rebecca said.

"It should be normal," Matthew said as he drove away.

18

DANE

Too loud for words, the boat sped toward land on the opposite shore. Dane glanced at Angus's determined gaze. Beads of spray collected on her long sleeves, throwing a silver sheen across her arm, and Dane flashed on the lateral pull of the silver cord she drew across the neck of the man she'd hated for what seemed an eternity. It was done. It was over, though she pushed that revelation back and out of her mind for now.

Trembling to realize the killing of intended targets was complete, she was that much closer. She only dreamed she'd get this far. With two major hurdles down, she could close the distance, if it wasn't too late.

And just with that little doubt, Dane looked down, took a deep breath and forced herself again to look up. She took another breath and looked ahead. What she saw then made her glance at Angus like he was crazy. "We'll have to find another way. We can't go in there. Look at all the security. There must be some kind of riot."

He chuckled. "That's what I was about to suggest. That riot's likely led by my wife. We'd better hurry."

"Is she armed? Will she be okay a little while longer?"

"Oh, I'm not worried about her. I'm worried about anyone standing in her way." Angus chuckled again.

Dane smiled but then heard a noise over the din of the engine and when she turned, she saw a US Coast Guard 33-foot SAFE boat darting after them.

Angus followed her line of sight.

"Go, go, just keep going!" Dane yelled as Angus pulled away and aimed to the right. "Don't stop; they'll give up."

Angus looked behind them again and then let off the gas.

"I said don't stop!" Dane said, raising the gun.

"Don't point that thing at anyone! Are you crazy?"

"Keep going!" she said, and Angus sped up again, weaving along the shoreline without looking back.

Dane lowered the gun and whipped her hair out of her face while keeping an eye on the Coast Guard boat. "They're slowing. If they really wanted to, they would've overtaken us already. Instead, they're chasing us off."

"Why would they do that?"

She shook her head. "I don't know. Maybe it's policy not to let any boats make it into the harbor. We'll have to dock somewhere else. You're from the island...where do we go?"

He stood a little taller and looked toward shore. "Rolling Bay," he said. "We can get back in town from that way."

Dane watched behind them as the Coast Guard boat turned around. "It's likely they're not letting anyone near the ferry dock. I just need to get to the hardware store on 305. Do you know where that is?"

"Yes," he said. "My mate lives nearby. We might ask him for a ride if he's willing to get us that far. I can walk the rest of the way."

Dane cut an eye at him. "As long as you get me to my truck. That was the deal."

"Yeah. No problem. You'll get to your truck."

She watched his profile a while longer, until it was uncomfortable enough that he turned back to her.

"I gave you my word," he barked.

She didn't physically jump. That would show weakness on her part, but she wanted to. Never before had she been yelled at by a Scotsman. Though he seemed like any ordinary businessman on the surface, she detected a fierce temper that she'd prefer to keep on her good side.

When she looked to the shoreline on the right the contrast with the city view seared on her memory. To the starboard side, a raven's wing. To the port, a bluebird's. Where they met in the middle, a jaggedness, as if heaven and hell were ripping the sky apart at the seams.

She looked back at the house-lined street. They seemed like play homes in some train model's scene. The closer their approach, the more detailed. A little window outlined in with peeling teal paint. A prison-like metal-framed house the color of a mourning soul. A long-eroded sidewalk. A decades-old pier barely hanging on. The remnants of another pier from the distant past jutted from the water. Cars parked on one end of the long street in a huddle. Little boats bobbing on the waves connected to ball-shaped orange buoys. A few stick figures lined up like pillars on a concrete promenade, shielding their eyes with one hand.

"We won't make it to shore," Angus was saying but Dane had not yet given up on the images before her. Tearing herself away from the scene she said finally, "What do you mean?"

"Wrong kind of boat. We can't run it up on the beach. See that boat there?" he pointed. "We can get to the buoy and paddle the rest of the way ashore."

"Where does he live?"

"Who?"

"Your...mate."

Angus bobbed his chin out toward the right far end of the street where it ended.

"Great. Are you sure he's home?"

"He's home; that's him. Right there." Angus pointed to one of the taller thin figures on the horizon.

This time, it was Dane who shielded her eyes and peered out at the tall, dark-haired man. He stood near the shore. And as if the guy read their minds, he turned and ran away back to the front of his house and pulled out a red kayak and hauled it to the water's edge and began paddling like mad to his boat.

"What's he doing?" Dane asked.

Angus chuckled. "He can't tell it's me from here, so he's either going to help us or hurt us. He's sees that we're going for his boat."

Dane watched the man. "He can die trying," she said and gripped the butt of her gun a little bit tighter.

"Hey," Angus yelled out at the man and raised his arm.

"Why are you slowing down?" Dane asked.

"Because he's in a kayak and I don't want to blow him over."

"Why not?"

"Because you get more with honey than you do with vinegar. Hasn't anyone taught you that?"

Dane let the question hang there.

Angus scoffed. "Of course not. Your only answer is a gun."

"Hey," Dane said and meant it as a warning. "If it was someone else stealing our boat, I'm sure you'd think differently. Now tell your *mate,* to give us a ride."

Angus looked at her. "I will not *tell* him to give us a ride. I will *ask* him. John," Angus yelled, waving his arm again. "John, it's me."

The dark-haired man looked up as he scooted from his

kayak to his boat strapped to a buoy. "Angus!" he said, his expression drawn in confusion. "You stole a whole freaking ferry?" John said as their boat sidled up to his boat. "I'm pretty sure there are laws against that, man. Who's the chick?"

Dane didn't say a word and hid the gun down by her side, but noted this new stranger gave her a lingering suspicious look. He wasn't smiling and whipped his too-long hair to the side to get a better look at her. He was an attractive older guy, all scruffy dark beard with gray showing through. If anything, he reminded her of Professor Snape, only better looking.

She broke the trance he held on her when the Scottish accent began to speak again. "We borrowed it. But now we need a ride. Can you help us out?"

"Who's this?" John asked.

She was going to speak...say that her name was Dane and she was her own personal vigilante assassin, but Angus broke in and said, "This is my friend. She's commuted with me for years. She needs to get back to the hardware store but her ankle's busted."

"Ouch does your friend have a name?" John said.

"Dane," she said before Angus could answer.

"Can we tie up your taxi here? I mean, I'm sure whoever you borrowed it from will find it. There's satellite tracking devices on these things."

Both Dane and Angus sat up a little straighter.

"Best we leave it intact for the owners to pick it up then," Angus said. "Can you stand?"

Angus held out an arm for her to grab onto, but Dane refused and pushed herself up using the back of the seat but sat down hard again.

"Stop being so stubborn," Angus said.

John interrupted and jutted his chin out. "You guys better

hurry up. I think the owner of your boat is coming to collect his toy, and he doesn't look too happy."

"Oh, they're not going to give up after all," Angus said.

Red lights and sirens were beating a wake toward them. This time Angus didn't ask; he just yanked Dane up by the forearm and drug her to the edge of the boat.

She winced in pain and realized her ankle had time to swell in the last half hour.

"We're not going to outrun them in this boat, but we can at least create some space," John said and then stared hard at Dane when he saw the gun.

"Unless of course you're going to start a shootout. Put that away before someone sees it," John warned.

"Drop it in the water," Angus urged.

"Let's not be crazy," John said.

Dane was never going to listen to either of them, but she did keep her weapon out of sight as they got into the boat.

Dane took one last look over her shoulder as the boat arced a deadly path toward them and forgot all about her ankle as she leapt into John's boat.

"Go, go, go," Angus yelled.

John took off and as Dane leaned into her seat, she and Angus kept an eye on the coming boat.

"Don't worry. They don't want you. They just want the boat," John said, and he was right. As the cruiser neared, they slowed to a stop.

"See?" John said, staring at Dane. "Nothing to worry about."

"Can you just get us to the hardware store?" Angus said. "The sooner I get her on her way, the better."

Dane looked at the two of them. The last thing she wanted was to get more people involved in her troubles. She needed to get back to her truck and put some distance between herself and anyone who recognized her. There was more she needed to accomplish and the less time she spent with anyone who could point her out in a lineup, the better.

John nodded once and aimed toward shore.

19

MATTHEW

"We are never getting through this snarly mess. Owen, can you pull up Maps?" Lee said.

Matthew had his head hovered over the new phone in the passenger seat. "I don't get this damn thing. This is like no other phone I've ever seen. There's no actual buttons to push. It's just a dark, flat screen. What am I doing wrong?"

"Is there a manual? Did he give us one in here?" Owen said.

Holding the display closer, Matthew said, "Oh wait...I see a little green light. I'm assuming it's her. Or else this stranger is leading us into a trap."

"Why would he give us a tricked-out vehicle?" Owen said. "I haven't even figured out all the buttons on the dashboard yet," he said, hovering a finger over a grayed-out rectangle.

"Don't touch that," Rebecca said. "We don't know what it will do."

Talking over their banter, Matthew said, "Because generally bad guys try to frame innocent guys for their own crimes."

"Yeah, we're not getting through this," Lee said, gripping the steering wheel and reminding them of the jammed traffic ahead and then everyone took their eyes off their own devices and stared at the screen on the dashboard in front of them because it suddenly turned on by itself and the stranger with the motorcycle from before appeared and used his thumb to point up.

"Turn it up. He's trying to talk to us," Rebecca said. And because they all sat there without moving, she huffed and leaned between the seats and with her outstretched hand she turned the volume up herself.

"Hello," Nehale said.

"Can you hear us?" Matthew said.

The man smiled slightly as if to say, *Of course.*

"Good." Matthew flipped the mysterious phone around. "I'm assuming this is Dane's location and that's where we're supposed to find her. That doesn't make sense because she was in the hospital last time I checked and now you're saying she's on the Kitsap Peninsula? And by the way, how do you operate this thing? Is this some new operating system?"

Nehale nodded with the same slight smile as before without explaining.

"I thought they'd stopped the ferries," Lee said.

Nehale shrugged. "She found a different way. And had assistance from a few new friends. Listen, you need to meet up with her in Tacoma after she gets over the Narrows Bridge. Don't go over the Narrows though. Stay on the Tacoma side. Do you understand?"

"Uh," Lee said. "It doesn't look like we're going anywhere near Tacoma or any bridge anytime soon. Can you see a big red line on your map there?"

Matthew showed Lee the screen on the phone without saying a word.

"You tell me, man. Have you ever seen anything like this?"

Lee hovered his finger over the phone. "Can you tap it or expand it? Use your finger."

"Gentleman," Nehale said, drawing their attention to the

main screen on the dashboard once more. "You are getting out of here, I can assure you. As soon as this call ends, follow the directions on the map feed that follows. You'll have no problems. The map will guide you through the back streets and we'll monitor your progress. If we see anything standing in your way, we'll take care of it ahead of time and redirect you accordingly. Do not lose the phone."

"We?" Rebecca whispered loudly. "Who's *we*, Matthew?"

With a deadpan expression, Matthew used one level hand and motioned from the backseat to the front. "What she just said. Who's *we* and more to the point, *who* the hell are *you*?" Matthew asked.

"I'm also a friend of Dane's and you can call me Nehale."

Pointing to his chest, Matthew said, "*I'm* a friend of Dane's. She's never mentioned you."

"Mr. Brogen, what matters now..."

"Ooh," Rebecca whispered. "He called you Mr. Brogen."

Nehale smiled then continued. "What matters now is that you intercept Ms. Talbot as soon as possible. She's going to need all the assistance she can get now. You've already committed to help her, correct?"

Silence. Then, "I thought the hard part was over," Matthew said.

"How does *he* know that?" Rebecca whispered again.

"Shh," Lee said.

The phone suddenly buzzed in Matthew's hand, causing him to look down at the screen.

"See the marker on the map that's moving toward the Agate Pass bridge off Bainbridge Island to Poulsbo?"

The screen zoomed wide on its own. "Wait, how did you do that?"

Ignoring the question, Nehale said, "Do you see the bridge, Mr. Brogen?"

"Yes," he barked then added under his breath, "Call me Matthew."

"Dane's going to have trouble there because the islanders have long decided to blockade the bridge in the event of an emergency situation to conserve their own resources."

Lee said, "Well, that's shooting yourself in the leg if you ask me."

Nehale smiled through the slight interruption as if he agreed then continued, "Yes, well...that's not our concern. Getting her over the bridge to the other side is our mission. If you continue to watch the live screen, you'll see in a few moments...there..." he continued.

Owen had leaned over the seat to watch the screen, huddled with the others. "Whoa, look at that guy go. They're pushing that truck out of the way. Those people are tiny."

Matthew ignored Owen's words but lifted his eyes directly at Owen and Lee as if in a private huddle then broke away. It was a moment he needed without looking at Nehale—and then he realized everything. Now he understood what was really going on.

"Nehale, I think we grasp the situation," Matthew said and swallowed. "How about we get to work. Get us out of here. Like you said, we have a mission."

Nehale smiled with his eyes in that same way again and nodded slightly. "Understood," he said. "In a few minutes, you'll notice a clearing ahead of you and the map will open on the screen as well. We're always monitoring but if you need assistance and we don't hear you, use your thumbprint on the center of the phone's screen for a few seconds."

"Hmm...well, ain't that something. You recorded my fingerprint without authorization."

Nehale's smile broadened. "We don't work on *authorizations*, Mr. Brogen. I'm sure you realize that by now."

Matthew's eyebrows raised, and he smiled back at him. "Oh, I do get that, now. Hey, before you go, do me a favor and tell *Paul* I said hi!"

20

DANE

Since arguing with strangers wasn't exactly the goal she had in mind for the day, Dane kept quiet. *Just get to the truck,* she kept saying to herself. That is, until she decided they weren't doing anything right.

John was arguing with Angus about how to land the boat on the shore at a high rate of speed.

"You have to go faster," John said, "or it won't moor right."

"We'll break our necks!" Angus yelled.

"Let me do it," John said, trying to wrench the wheel away.

It wasn't exactly the type of boat you'd run up on shore. But they had no choice; the shoreline was approaching like a freight train and the boat was speeding up, and there was no stopping now. And as the guys argued over who was going to steer and how fast they'd go, Dane couldn't help but shout, "Hold on," and braced herself, as they crashed with a crunch and spray of gravel and lurched hard forward and then, mercifully, snapped back again.

Too stunned to move at first, Dane finally put her foot down, the wrong foot.

"I can't believe you did that," yelled John after a pause.

"I didn't do that. You did," Angus shouted back with the veins in his neck protruding.

"I'm fine. Thank you," Dane said, but neither heard her over their shouting match. "Both of you shut up. Where's the car?" Dane said.

Turning to her, John said, "I suppose you still want me to drive you to into town now that you broke my boat."

"I did not break your boat," Angus said and looked from Dane to John again. "It's fine, see?" he said, after jumping to shore and inspecting the damage on his side.

"It's scratched all to hell," John said from the other side, kneeling down with his shoes crunching in the gravel to inspect the damage.

Dane didn't interject in their conversation, but she gave Angus a long stare while John was still knelt down on the other side.

He got the message.

"John...can you please get us to her truck now? I know it's a lot to ask..." Angus said, staring straight at Dane and not John.

When John stood up, he eyed him and then he eyed her and dropped the menacing look on his face, replacing it with a crooked smile.

"What kind of trouble does she have you in, Angus?" he looked to Dane. "You're not his type...but you're pregnant, aren't you?"

She nearly snorted.

"There's no trouble. My God, Jacqui'd kill me. It's nothing like that," Angus said. "I just need to get her back to her truck."

John looked suspicious but nodded. "I agree. It's nothing like that, but there is something. What kind of trouble have you gotten dear Angus into, darling?"

She didn't answer.

"Just get us to her truck, will you? Stop asking questions we can't answer," Angus said.

John brightened. "Excellent. Danger and intrigue. A femme fatale. Let's get going. No dawdling, my dear." He lifted a hand to help her out of the boat.

Ignoring him, she braced herself and stood, placing most of her weight on the non-shattered ankle and hiding the pain from her features.

"My, you are a stubborn one," John said.

She wasn't sure how much he was joking or if there was sincerity in his voice. She felt him staring at her as she pulled herself to the side of the boat and gingerly lifted one leg over the edge.

"I can do it myself," she said when he attempted to brace her landing.

"Alrighty, then," he said. Then, "Come on, Angus. Why are you taking so long?"

They left her there to follow them even as the lapping water reached her heels. She took one step and immediately regretted refusing the helping hands but then again, she had to get through this. She found her old resolve by placing one foot in front of the other and carefully placing her weight on her ankle, finding it easier to brace her weight on the ball of her foot instead of the heel. She continued that way up the beach through the shifting pebbles. She followed their silent lead and detected Angus looking back at her to make sure she was keeping pace, while she also noticed John did not check back—or she never caught him looking.

And just like a training run with a hangover in Montana hills with Tuck yelling at you, she kept herself walking through the pain behind them for another block as her mind kept flashing back to Matthew. She so much wished he was there.

"Not much farther," John said, with a backward glance when

she began to falter, sweat pouring down her back. She lifted her chin.

After a while longer she said, "How much further?" She could endure the feeling of grinding bones with the nerve fibers crunching between them if only she knew how much longer it would take until the pain would cease. Otherwise, she couldn't take another step, her foot lifted above the other, unwilling to descend again.

John turned suddenly and seethed, "Will you just let us help you? My God, woman! Just knock it off."

He reached for her.

She automatically took a step back, but she wasn't fast enough, and he had a grip on her forearm and jerked her forward but braced her before she landed on her ankle.

"Here Angus, get on the other side. We'll just walk her the rest of the way to the car. Don't attempt to argue, Dane if that's your real name."

Too stunned he didn't think her name was her real name, she ignored that and concentrated on placing her weight on their shoulders while she hobbled between them. And then that was it. Flanked by both men, she made it another half a block and there they stood in front of his little white car in a tiny parking lot at the base of a hilled road.

"We're supposed to all fit in here?" Dane asked.

John grunted.

Angus chucked.

"Is that a Porsche? Why would you have a Porsche during the apocalypse?" Dane asked.

"No one sent me the notice we were entering an apocalypse," John said.

Dane nodded. "That writing's been on the wall for a while now. You should read occasionally."

"I'm retired from society. I don't give a damn what they do to one another. It's only when the mayhem spills over into my life that's the problem...like today, for instance," he said with a smile. "That's when I get pissed off. Otherwise, I'm happy to ignore it all and drive fast down twisted roads."

As soon as the door closed, John sped away, flinging gravel into the air as he roared up the hill and pushed his way through the coiled roads at a reckless speed, pushing Dane hard into the seat.

However, as soon as they turned left on the highway, they realized there was going to be a problem. What looked like a long, one-lane traffic back-up was actually delayed ferry passenger parking, but it never ended. It snaked the entire length of the island, all the way to the Agate Pass bridge between there and the Kitsap Peninsula.

"Great...idle hands make riot gods great," John said.

"Where'd you get that? Is it some kind of allegory" asked Angus.

"Nah...I just made it up," John said.

"Quite prophetic," Angus said.

When September Ends by Green Day blared through the speakers suddenly and John turned up the volume with a press on his steering wheel button as he steered between people wandering around on the empty lane like refugees, walking around aimlessly in the middle of the highway. The few that they passed looked as if they were begging for a fight. They wanted someone to blame. They had that edgy look about them. Like a parent without coffee first thing in the morning after a long, hectic night, nothing good was going to come of this.

"Jeez," John said.

"Avoid that one," Angus yelled over the music and pointed out an older man up ahead with a long beard and a belly just as long hanging over his worn jeans, staring them down.

"You think?" John said rhetorically.

As John slowly maneuvered around him, the man took a step out in front of him. And then John began to speed a little faster when the guy used his beefy hand to slam down on the roof of his car as he passed. They were all silent for a moment, but then John laughed, "I could've taken him."

Dane chuckled, and she caught John smiling at her in the rear view mirror as they all chuckled over the tense situation.

"Tell me why I'm doing this again?" John said after he turned the music down an octave.

"Because we're mates." Angus said with a sly smile.

"Oh, that's right. I remember that now that there's a large fist-size dent in the top of my car." John pointed with one finger up and then lazily laid the others over the steering wheel comfortably as if he wasn't nervous about the people meandering through the street. "Just to the hardware store, right?"

"Yes, that's right," Dane said, when Angus didn't answer. "That's all I need. Just get me to the hardware store and that'll work." But then she suddenly yelled, "Stop."

"Why?" Angus said.

"I don't have the keys," she said. "I lost the backpack."

"No. Your backpack's right there," Angus said.

"No. I lost the original backpack," she said, not taking the time to explain the last twenty-four hours. It was difficult to remember all the events that recently happened herself, let alone having to explain them to someone else and there—well, there was the murder. "I don't have the damn keys to the truck. That's the point."

"All right. Don't get upset. What does that mean? What do we need to do?" John said. "Do I turn around?"

"No! We are not turning around. Let me out here if you're going to turn around," Angus said.

"Hold on," Dane said, not believing what she was about to do, and dug the phone out of the backpack Nehale gave her earlier. "Let me make a call first." There was only one phone number listed on the mysterious phone. And when the ringing stopped, someone answered, the voice was the same guy as before. She didn't know what else to say and blurted out, "I don't have the keys to the truck," hoping he knew what she was talking about.

After a pause and in a calm voice Nehale said, "You're in a vehicle now and it's moving as far as we can tell. Can you get to Tacoma on your own or do you need assistance?" he said.

She held the phone away from her and looked at it quizzically, and then put it back to her ear. "I don't know, let me find out." Lowering the phone so that he couldn't hear the conversation, Dane looked at John and said, "Is there any way you can get me to Tacoma?"

John raised his eyebrows at her without answering.

Angus interrupted the silence and said, "*I'm* not going to Tacoma. I am going as far as the hardware store. That was our deal. I can walk back into town from there. But I'm not going to Tacoma; I'm not leaving the island."

John had not taken his eyes off her. He seemed to be contemplating something and chewed on the inside of his cheek.

Angus began to say something else, but John lifted his hand. "That's all right, Angus, I'll get you to Jacqui." And then he looked back at Dane. "You're asking me to drive an hour's journey, on a good day, in a dented sports car through an apocalypse, and I don't even know you, darling."

She held his stare a beat and then said, "It's fine." She dismissed the idea and pulled the stranger on the phone back to her ear.

"Wait," John said, "I need to go to Bremerton anyway to check on my mother. I'll take you to Tacoma and check on her on the way back. You're lucky, Dane Talbot. Listen, I don't know you and I don't know who you have on the other end of that phone, but you might want to make sure they're not trying to get you killed."

She agreed with him. She couldn't trust anyone. She was taking chances now, reckless ones, but she had no choice either. There was only one thing that mattered now above all else, and the time for safety was gone. She had to act and she had to act now. If anyone got in her way, they were going down since she only had one thing to lose and too much distance in between. It was she who was likely to get herself killed trying to do what she needed to do. They were just helping her...whoever *they* were. But instead, she said, "Thank you," because explaining the rest was too much to do when she needed to be somewhere else. Even the *Thank you* stuck in her throat and John chuckled a little to himself as he maneuvered back onto the roadway. Somehow she amused him.

"Our first mission is to deliver Angus to Jacqui," John said and sped away.

Dane held the stranger on the phone to her ear once again and said, "I have a ride."

"Affirmative, let us know if you need anything else or if you get into a bind," Nehale said.

"Why are you doing this?" Dane asked.

"That's not a question that I can answer, Ms. Talbot," Nehale said.

Dane said, "Who can?"

A pause. "I can only say that I don't have the authority to answer that question, Ms. Talbot."

Dane swallowed the lump forming in her throat. Lowering her voice so that John and Angus could not hear her words, she said, "Not one soul in the world is aware of my mission. I've not told anyone."

"Ms. Talbot, I can only say you are not alone," Nehale said. "But what I can tell you, is this: You *are* pressed for time. Check the news at your earliest convenience. It seems the bill has passed despite all opposition."

A shaky finger ended the call. And despite all the danger Dane had ever faced in her life, now was the time her hands trembled like they never had before.

21

MATTHEW

I t had only been half an hour but, Lee said, "I can't believe this guy's going so fast. I've never seen anyone drive back roads like this before. We're in a neighborhood one second. And then we're back on the highway weaving between cars the next."

Rebecca said from the back seat, "I wouldn't be surprised if they use the helicopter and transport us next. And in this kind of traffic, they might have to."

"Who's this Paul guy, anyway?" Owen said. "Isn't that the guy, Matthew...the one that you said died?"

He stopped when Matthew interrupted him. "I was just taking a stab in the dark. Yes, that's the guy. He's the founder of Rebel Blaze. An old friend of Dane's and he's supposed to be dead." Matthew chuckled. "At least, that's what I'm guessing."

Owen said, "Well, he's clearly not dead and he's got to be loaded. I mean, this has to cost a fortune. Or someone's got a great trust fund with a butler and services."

"Hold up, we're slowing down a bit here," Lee said, flexing his white-knuckled fingers, "which is fine by me. Driving like a junky on his last hit is making me nervous, and that's saying something for a smokejumper." He pulled into a parking lot behind the lead vehicle while opening and closing his fists to relieve the tension.

"Where are we?" Matthew said.

Rebecca read the sign. "War Memorial Park. Answer it, Matthew."

Matthew shook his head and fumbled for the phone, seeing Nehale's image on the screen.

When he picked up, Nehale said, "You need to turn it off mute. You need to keep the volume up at all times."

"Well, how the hell do you do that? There are no buttons on this damn thing," Matthew barked.

"Just hit the left side of the screen with your finger and slide up," Nehale explained.

And that's when Matthew realized the screen *was* the touch pad, with all the inherent buttons. "Oh, I'll be damned."

"We've hit a little delay," Nehale said. "Dane is temporarily detained, but she'll be along shortly. Please wait at the rendezvous area. While you're waiting, you might look over the route to your next destination. This will get you where you need to go with all the stops along the way."

"Is she okay? Is Dane all right?" Matthew asked, trying to keep the panic out of his voice.

Nehale calmly smiled, setting him at ease. "Yes, she's fine. We've had a slight change in plans that's going to cause a minor delay. Nothing to worry about. You're in a safe spot to wait for her. And we will make sure she gets to you."

"Who says *rendezvous* anymore?" Owen whispered from the backseat, his mouth twisted at one end.

"O-kay," Lee said, drawing the words out.

Nehale continued, "While you're waiting for Dane, we'll take the opportunity to go over some plans concerning your trip. Once you have Dane en route nearby we'll let you know."

"What do you mean our next destination?" Matthew said. "Where are we going?"

Nehal did that damn calm smile, as if all was right in the world, again. "That will be revealed to you soon. For now you don't really need that information."

"Ooh, a mystery," Rebecca said.

Owen chuckled and said, "You're so damn cute," and then there were smooching sounds in the backseat.

Matthew couldn't help but roll his eyes. At least they kept the lovey-dovey stuff to themselves. Most of the time.

"Can we not do that right now, you guys?" Matthew whispered in a harsh tone behind him.

"Oh...okay," Owen said. "Right, understood."

"For now, I want you to understand there are a few events taking place that might complicate our plans. Have you looked at the latest news broadcast?" Nehale said.

For the second time in the last three minutes, Matthew shook his head and rolled his eyes at the same time but for different reasons.

Nehale nodded. "You might take a look while you're waiting. Keep abreast of what obstacles might stand in your way."

"Right. Well, how'm I suppose to know that when I don't even know our next destination? And since it seems there are no costs expended for this mission of Dane's, why not just charter a helicopter to get her there faster? Why the tricked-out ride?" Matthew said.

"Because all air space has been shut down. There's a no-fly zone over the entire United States and Canada," Nehale said.

All Matthew could say then was, "Damn."

"But you could do that if you wanted to, I bet," Owen said. "The helicopter and private jet thing?"

"Yes," Nehale said. "It's a complicated situation, but there are ways around complications when deadlines approach. I suggest you look over the upcoming travel plans while you wait." And with that, Nehale ended the call.

"Calm man," Lee said under his breath. "You want to drive at the speed of sound, and I'll deal with the pleasant little man on the tiny screen? I'll trade you, seriously."

Matthew turned to him.

It's a known fact that a death stare delivers a frosty chill.

22

DANE

"What does that mean?" John said, alternately weaving his way through obstacles in the roadway and looking to her for some kind of clarification.

She stared straight through the windshield for a moment.

"What does that mean?" John repeated a little louder.

"You can drop me off here," Angus said from the backseat. "This is far enough. I can walk the rest of the way."

"I can get you to the intersection at least," John yelled.

"No, you don't have to," Angus said and took off his seatbelt. "Pull over."

"It's not much farther, Angus. Just wait a minute," John said.

But then Dane braced herself because Angus had grabbed the back of her seat and yelled, "I said, pull the bloody car over! Why don't you goddamn well listen? Let me out."

Dane looked at John, who had not only pulled over but raised his eyebrows. "Don't piss off the Scottish man," John mumbled to himself as he neared the shoulder of the roadway that wasn't occupied by refugees waiting impatiently for a ferry-boat that wasn't coming.

When the Porsche stopped, Dane quickly checked her surroundings and then opened the door and stepped out.

Angus flew out of the backseat, his face flushed red hot. "I don't know what you've got yourself into, but you need to be careful with the lives you destroy in your wake."

He turned and walked down the side of the median then without another word, before she got a chance to say anything. She closed her mouth. He was right, after all. She'd known that. She was destroying the lives of those she came across. Using them to get where she needed to go. The father, Waylan, came to mind. She felt bad for causing him trouble but then again, her mind flashed on her ultimate goal and that image disappeared in a flash.

"Get in. He'll get over it," John said.

She watched Angus's retreating form for a while but then tore herself away. Nope, she didn't feel a thing. Time to get back on the road.

Back inside the vehicle, she slammed the door.

"Easy, darling," John said as he made a wide U-turn around the roamers in the street.

"Don't worry about him. He'll forget all about it in time; he's a Scotsman."

Not that she cared, but in an attempt to make conversation, she said, "Are they known for their forgiveness?" Because she didn't think that was the case.

John chuckled. "Oh hell no. *You'll* never be friends with him again. I just mean he'll forget you ever existed...not that he'll forgive your sins. Ha-ha."

She could only nod and agree that it didn't matter. She wasn't surviving to make friends.

The rumble of the engine told her that John was picking up speed while she fumbled through the phone in an attempt to pull up a browser. She needed to research the best way to get there and see what stood in her way, but she also wanted to see what Nehale might be talking about. It truly was her worst nightmare coming true that the bill was passing, and she had little time left.

And just pulling up the world news showed her the headlines across the country: *DNA Release Gives New Insight into Crash 542*. Another one read... *Solved! Long time suspect is Kennedy Killer. No More Deadbeat Dads in less than 48 Hours.*

Then she looked up Bill's name and so far, there was no mention of his untimely death. But his mother *was* mentioned. She was mentioned a lot and she was very much alive.

Senator Mathus Accused of Cover-Up, Mathus Heads FREE DNA Release Commission, President-Elect orders Review of Senator Maria Mathus' Finances, State Seeks Mathus Indictment, Mathus Under Scrutiny in Alleged Assassination Attempt... Mathus tied to Chicago Fires.

If her hands were shaking before she read the latest headlines, the cadence had tripled then, and the clock was ticking faster now. Dane knew she was a step ahead, but it wouldn't be long before Mathus would know her name, too.

23

MATTHEW

Lee flicked a finger at the lead vehicle parked in front of them. "Is he going to wait here the whole time with us? I mean, what's the point? Why doesn't he just hit the highway and retrieve Dane himself?"

"Man, I don't know. There're a few things about this whole thing that don't make any sense to me," Matthew said and then the phone in his hand pinged and the screen on the dashboard lit up again, this time with a map. "Here we go," Matthew said.

Lee scrolled the map closer in by widening two fingers over the screen. "You don't actually have to touch the screen, Lee. It can feel your body temperature inches away; you can just open your fingers," Owen said from the back seat.

"How do you know that?" Lee asked.

"Because there's another screen back here on the back of your seat," Owen said.

"Why didn't you say so?" Matthew said, peering around to the back seat.

"Thought you knew—look," Owen said and had his hand over ten inches away from the map on the screen and opened and closed his thumb and forefinger to show the map expanding and contracting.

Matthew couldn't believe his eyes. Then he looked back at Lee and saw that he was now doing the same thing. "I wonder what else this thing can do. It's probably scanning our vitals while we sit here."

"I'm sure we don't want to know," Lee said.

Matthew looked at the phone in his hand and tapped the blue file icon presented on the screen.

"Where are we going, Matthew?" Rebecca asked as she hovered over the back of his seat, looking over his shoulder.

He trailed the long highlighted dark blue line all the way down and said at last, "Texas."

"Well, that's going to be tricky. They closed the border a few days ago," Owen said, "according to the news I see here. Texas Rangers and armed citizens all along the border."

Lee said, "You mean the Mexican border?"

"No. I mean the state border all along the panhandle and all the other angled lines," Lee said. "It had something to do with preserving the pipeline from anarchists and vandalism."

Matthew read further. "We're headed to a little town outside of Corpus Christi called Tivoli."

"That's a long way from here, man," Lee said as if the journey was impossible, and Matthew lowered the phone and said, "Listen, guys, if you want to quit, now's the time. No hard feelings. That goes for all of you."

Everyone stared from one to the next for a silent beat.

"Hey, I didn't say I wanted to quit," Lee said, raising his voice.

"What the hell, Matt? We're going. No one's quitting," said Owen.

And then suddenly, the lead vehicle in front of them started up and peeled away, exiting the empty parking lot in a flash.

"What the hell just happened?" Owen said as they watched.

"There's someone coming up behind us," Rebecca said suddenly.

24

DANE

The winding road ahead led to the Agate Pass Bridge. Dane saw it there beyond the barricade. Beyond a group of people standing in the way holding onto signs at the ends of sticks like the ones she'd seen many times on the news. But these were not protest signs. These signs were warning signs. *Bridge is Closed. Save our Island.*

"Nut jobs," John mumbled under his breath as he pressed down on the accelerator.

Dane pushed herself farther into the seat and held tighter to the armrest. "Is there another way?" was all she got out before the people scattered and John plowed through a plastic barricade blocking his path, sending him skidding to the side where one glimpse out of Dane's window showed her exactly how far it would be to fall into the hard waves below. But it wasn't the slide that scared her. John regained control of the wheel pretty quickly and turned the car around. What scared her was the way he was laughing the entire time they nearly lost their lives. A maniacal chuckle that sent shivers up her spine. He was enjoying this, as if it was the first time he'd lived in the last several years.

"You realize you've smashed up your fancy car."

"It already had a fist-sized dent in the roof today. I'll get another one," he chuckled again and began weaving between the oncoming vehicles passing him by to take advantage of the opening he'd created.

"It's insane that they even barricaded the bridge. Why do that? Why isolate yourself from the mainland?" Dane asked.

John shook his head. "You can't teach stupid. You're born with it."

Which really made no sense to her, but she wasn't going to argue with him. They continued to accelerate up the hill to the other side of the bridge into the town of Poulsbo, where traffic began to thicken again.

"You might want to pull up a map or something. We may need..." John said but they were interrupted by Dane's phone and the same man who'd rescued her earlier in the day appeared on the screen.

"Dane," Nehale smiled. "I see you've crossed the bridge onto the Kitsap Peninsula, and your group is awaiting your arrival once you cross the Narrows Bridge. An escort car will join you soon to help you navigate through the crowded streets. There will be some unconventional paths."

"Why do we need an escort car?" John said.

"Shh," Dane said.

Nehale smiled slightly again. "He will intervene in case you have any more trouble."

"Ahh," John said. "He doesn't like my reckless driving."

Ignoring him, Dane said, "Wait, you said my *friends* were waiting for me? Who exactly are we talking about?"

"Matthew and his group. You were aware they were waiting to join you?"

"I...I thought it was just going to be Matthew. I don't want to involve anyone else in this. I don't even want him involved."

"Involved in what?" John said.

"Shh," she said again.

Nehale's slight smile became a straight line. "Might I suggest that this is a time when you cannot have too many friends, Ms. Talbot. Especially those who are willing to risk a bit of danger. Your journey, as you know, is a long one. You're going to need the help of many."

She didn't like this, but she also didn't see a way around it either.

"Why are you here, Nehale? At first I thought it was Matthew somehow, but now I'm suspecting something crazy."

Nehale looked down suddenly and pressed something closer to his ear and nodded his head. Then his speech picked up quickly. "Unfortunately, there's no time to explain. Please have your driver pick up speed *now*. There's a hijacked military convoy coming up quickly behind you."

"Where?" John said, looking in the rear-view mirror.

"Do you see the black Challenger in front of you?" Nehale asked.

"Yes," they both yelled.

"Follow it now," Nehale yelled.

The black car ripped through a grassy median and John followed, his arms shaking like a tree limb in a typhoon as he tried to hold onto the steering wheel and keep up with the black Challenger. "Bloody hell..." John's voice reverberated as they hung on. "Does he realize I'm in a sports car not an SUV?"

Dane didn't care to answer as they fishtailed onto a one-way side road. Once the tires met the pavement and gained traction, the Porsche found its grip again and caught up to the black Challenger in no time.

25

MATTHEW

Matthew's eyes hit the passenger window mirror, only to be blinded by approaching high beams.

"Are we armed? Is there a firearm in here anywhere?" Owen said, searching frantically.

"Why do we have to be armed?" Rebecca said, slamming shut various compartments that Owen had opened.

Lee shielded his eyes and said, "It could be Dane."

"It's not Dane," Matthew said. "Someone got out and it's definitely not Dane. They're coming this way."

"Where's that Nehale guy?" Rebecca whispered. "He could tell us who this guy is."

"Nehale's never there when you need him. He just shows up when least expected," Owen said, pulling a wrench out of a toolbox.

"We've only known him for like a day," Rebecca said.

"Can you both quit it?" Matthew said. "He's coming this way."

"Who?" Rebecca said and then there was a tap on Lee's window.

"What? Do I roll it down?" Lee said.

"Yes," Matthew said. "Slowly."

Lee pressed the button and lowered the window as Matthew watched.

"Yes, officer?" Lee said, and Matthew breathed an inner sigh of relief.

"You can't park here. What are you up to?" the officer asked, flicking on a flashlight and beaming it past their faces.

"We were just taking a moment to check our map, officer. We're not staying. We were just trying to find an alternate route. We're firefighters from Montana. Not familiar with the area and the traffic is relentless."

The officer nodded his head and supposed their story washed since Matthew and the others were still dressed in their various firefighter shirts.

"I didn't know they issued tricked-out SUVs in Montana. Where'd you guys get hold of this thing?"

"We were given the vehicle after our truck was damaged in Seattle," Matthew said.

"Yeah, it's rough over there. Well, there's no way around the spaghetti bowl at the moment. You're not far off from the Spokane Exit, though. You'll have to just get in line like everyone else, I suppose."

"Thanks, officer. We were just taking a minute to regroup."

"Understood," he said. "Carry on."

They watched as the officer walked back to his vehicle and Lee rolled up the window.

"Now what do we do? He's waiting for us to leave," Lee said.

"Go ahead and start it up. We'll circle around later and come back."

"He's monitoring this area. I don't think that's a good idea. We have to call Nehale and tell him we need an alternate meeting point."

26

DANE

It was starting to get dark. Dane wasn't sure what to expect when they got closer to Tacoma but there was little to no traffic on the forest-lined highway then. It would likely be a sea of headlights when they reached the other side.

"So, uh, what kind of danger are you in?" John asked.

"I'm not sure what you mean," Dane said.

"Well," he laughed. "I'm driving a sports car at a high rate of speed during a lockdown. I'd say I'm entitled to at least know what kind of crime you committed."

Crime? Dane thought. She had committed a crime but not one she'd ever admit to this stranger.

"I'm not the criminal here," she lied. "I'm just trying to protect someone and I'm the only one who can."

"Hmm," he said. "Sounds to me like you've got a few friends in high places willing to help you out."

"Not really," she said. "I don't know who that guy is," she pointed to the car ahead. "Or why exactly he's helping me out."

But that gave her an idea. She whipped out the phone and tried to type in Matthew's number. But the whole screen just shook a little.

"So you can't call out. Interesting."

Then the phone rang in her hand.

"Ms. Talbot, please continue to follow the lead car. It seems we've evaded the hijacked military vehicle. However, there's been a change in plans once more. It seems Matthew's team had to leave their position. They're finding a new location to wait for you shortly. I will text the directions as soon as they're available. Is your driver all right? Is there anything that you might need?" said Nehale.

"No, we're fine, thanks," Dane said.

Then Nehale nodded and the call simply ended.

The Porsche rumbled down the highway a little longer, leaving an uncomfortable silence.

"Who is this guy. *Is there anything you need?*" John mocked and laughed. "Like what? A cold beverage?"

Dane glared at him but then had to suppress a smile. It was a little funny.

"Like, how would that even work? He suddenly whips alongside us and rolls down the window at a high rate of speed to reveal a butler's uniform holding out a chilly La Croix on a silver platter?"

She detected a note of seriousness in his voice despite the banter. "What are you trying to say?" Dane asked.

"Why. Are. You. In. Danger?" John said with the same smirk on his face as before, but his eyes were dark and narrowing.

"It's better if you didn't know," Dane finally said and shifted her gaze out the window. "Look, if you want to pull over and let me out, it's okay. I'll find another way to get there."

"No, I'm not pulling out. I gave you my word. I'm just curious. You're in some kind of high-rated danger and I'm driving you to meet up with other people who are also in danger and I'm just curious when the bullets will start flying. I mean, why doesn't this guy in front of us pull over and take you to them? Have you asked yourself that?"

"He has other things to do. He's not a chauffeur."

"Well, all I'm saying is that you're in some kind of shit and I'm driving you, which puts me in the same boat...or car, as it were, and out of plain courtesy you might consider sharing, since you already shook up old Angus."

"I didn't shake him up. He was just going in the same direction."

"Ah, don't worry about Angus. He needed a little excitement in his life anyway. It's boring being Scottish."

"I wasn't worried," Dane said, then the phone dinged and when she looked down a map opened up. Using two fingers, she widened it to reveal a red blinking beacon. "This must be Matthew. It's not as far as we thought. He's meeting us before the Narrows Bridge now."

"Let me see, Tubby's Trail Dog Park—I know where that is."

"You have a dog?"

"No," he said and grinned at her. "Ex-girlfriend."

"Ah. Okay, how long will it take us?" Dane said.

"Another ten minutes or so. Are you in some kind of rush to be rid of me?"

"Yes," Dane said.

"Fair enough. Do you think our escort also has the directions?"

"I assume so," Dane said, staring at the car ahead of them. "Why is he still there? I mean, we know where we're going and it's not like there's anything going on here at the moment."

And just as she said that, the car accelerated and sped away.

"Do we...should we follow it?"

Dane shook her head. "Nope. Not unless Nehale gives us a heads-up."

She stared at the phone just in case he heard her.

"It is kind of like they're listening to our every word, isn't it?"

Changing the subject, Dane said, "So we're going to be there soon, and you can drop me off and then you're off to your mother's place, right?"

He nodded. "Yes, that's correct. I'm going to check in on my mother. Don't make fun of me."

"I...I think that's very good of you. Why would I make fun of you? That's what a good son should do in an apocalypse." *Why am I rambling on at ease with this guy?*

He flayed his hands out on top of the steering wheel. "Why would you call this the apocalypse? This is...just the sixties on steroids."

"Have you been to Chicago lately? Do you watch the news?"

He shook his head then but still held a smile. "Hell no."

"To which?"

"Both of those."

"Well, you're still a good son to make sure your mom is safe. Why don't you move her onto the crazy island with you?"

"Ha, because she'd get along too well with the locals. In fact, she'd lead the charge. Let's not encourage Mom."

Dane smiled. Somehow, she was making small talk. This setting was far too normal for her.

"And the news...why don't you at least keep abreast of the mayhem?"

"Doesn't concern me. If it's in my backyard...like today...then I'll deal with it. Life's too short to put up with it all."

"What will happen if the craziness in Seattle spills too much into your backyard? That could easily happen, you know. I rolled up on your shore today."

"I know, but Angus brought you. That's different. If that happens, I'll pick up my mom and put her into my plane kicking and screaming and fly away."

"You can fly?"

"I can fly."

"Too bad for you, there's a no-fly zone lately."

"Yeah...there're ways around that. It's just like stealing a foot ferry and being chased by the coast guard and using the disaster around you as a distraction."

Dane's brow furrowed. "Great minds..." she said under her breath.

27

MATTHEW

"Tubby's Trail Dog Park. Wish we had a dog. Oh look, the phone's lit up." Rebecca said. "Answer it, Matthew."

Rebecca's cheerful voice grated on Matthew's nerves. "How can you be so...excited?"

"I love dogs," Rebecca said.

"Hey, let's quiet down and keep an eye out. There's a few cars here. I bet they're doing the same thing we're doing," Lee said.

"Waiting for Dane? I doubt it," Owen said.

"No, they're likely taking a break and regrouping from the highway mess and trying to figure out how to get where they're going."

"Yeah, well, a cop like earlier is likely to show up and question everyone again. I'm surprised the last one let us go so easily," Lee said.

"I think they have better things to do," Owen said.

Matthew listened to them jabber while keeping watch out the window. Then the screen on his phone lit up and gave a tiny jolt. "Hey guys, look," he said.

"We're the blue dot," Rebecca said while a red dot came nearer and nearer.

"Is that...Dane?" Lee said.

Matthew looked up toward the entrance to the parking lot. They'd parked near the middle, their front aimed at the entrance.

"That...or we've just let someone set us up," Owen said.

"For what?" Rebecca asked.

"Shhh," Matthew said.

Lee said, "See, look, there's a car coming. A beat-up Porsche. Matthew, wait. Don't get out just yet."

But it was too late. He'd opened the door and slammed it shut.

Dane was in that wrecked car. He knew it. He could feel her nearby and by the looks of it, she'd been through hell.

He couldn't help it; he felt his boot heels eat the ground as he walked toward the car as it parked. He neared the door, but it opened on its own and out stepped a tall, thin man with dark hair. Definitely not Dane. His stomach balled up at once.

"What do you want?" the guy asked with a menacing frown.

"I'm here for my friend, Dane Talbot. Do you know where she is?"

"You're not even armed. What kind of protection can you provide? And you call yourself a friend?"

"Stop," Dane said, and Matthew spun around at the sound of her voice.

In the dark, she leaned against the hood of the car, bracing herself.

"Well, give her hand, you moron," the man said. "Don't just stand there."

Ignoring the older guy, he rushed to Dane. Though he was at a loss for words, he couldn't help but hold onto her tightly and looped her arm around his.

"I can walk, Matthew," she said.

The man on the other side of the car said, "No, she can't. Don't believe a word she says."

"Here, take my backpack," Dane said, handing it to him.

He slung one strap over his shoulder and wrapped an arm around her waist and began walking her toward the SUV when suddenly another truck pulled quickly into the parking lot and immediately, they saw the flashes of gunfire in the darkening sky. "Get out of your cars," came a voice over loudspeakers. And when no one moved right away, the guy standing in the back of the truck aimed and fired at a nearby Mazda, shattering the windshield and plunging rounds into the red hood of the car.

Matthew had pulled Dane back and down behind the Porsche. He wasn't sure where the driver was.

"John," Dane said, knowing he was exposed to the robbers.

Matthew looked underneath the car, expecting to see him lying down there in a pool of his own blood, but he wasn't there.

"Where'd he go?" Dane said.

But then Matthew had other concerns because they were firing again in a spray of bullets covering the parking lot, including the black SUV, but when he looked more closely, he noticed the bullets were ricocheting off the exterior of the car and unlike the rest of the windshields in the parking lot, theirs was unshattered. *Noted,* he thought. But then he looked into the vacated Porsche and eyed the push button. Hoping he could start the thing, he intended to ram to the gunman.

"Dane, wait here. I'll be right back," Matthew said, but she wouldn't let him go, instead she clung to his arm...more like held him down.

"I don't think so; you'll get your head blown off."

Then what sounded like a nearby explosion had him covering his ears. And when he looked at the assault vehicle, the gunman fell in a heap to the pavement below. The driver was also slumped over the steering wheel. They'd been shot from behind.

Matthew stood up and someone clapped at him. He shook his head. "It wasn't me," he said, standing there empty-handed, and then he looked behind him, where John stood at the open trunk of the Porsche, smiling with a shotgun in one hand.

28

DANE

No one checked on the injured or the dead. They just started their cars, or tried to, and beelined for the exit, swerving around the assault vehicle blocking the way.

"You might need this," John said and picked up the rifle from the dead guy on the ground and tossed it to Dane.

"I'm surprised you know how to handle a rifle, being a Porsche guy," Dane said.

"I surprise a lot of people," he said and opened the door of the truck, spilling the other guy out into the parking lot, where he pointed the end of his shotgun at him and kicked him a little with the tip of his shoe. "Dead."

"Well, he is missing half his head," Matthew said.

John looked at him. "Are you complaining?"

Matthew shook his head. "Not in the least."

"Good. Here, have his gun," John said and tossed a pistol his way. "Here's some extra ammo for you too. All right now, you should get out of here." He stepped into the driver's side of the truck.

"You're leaving your car here?" Dane asked, and Matthew took a step back, she assumed to give them some space.

He slipped his shotgun onto the seat of the truck. "What? Do you expect me to drive that wreck all the way back?" John said, smiling.

"John," Dane said. She'd never met anyone before who tried to appear as if life was always an adventure made just for him. "Thank you. I mean it."

He nodded then. "Oh, I see. This is heartfelt from the girl without a heart."

"Something like that," Dane said.

"Listen, Dane. Try not to get anyone nice killed, and I don't know what's eating you but give yourself a break. Okay? If you're ever down this way, *don't* stop by." He smiled again.

This time she smiled back as he backed up the truck, turned and sped away.

"You ready?" Matthew said as he came and stood beside her. "We should get going. It's dark and well, there're bodies on the ground.

Just then the SUV pulled up next to them and then two phones rang at the same time, lighting the darkness around them.

29

DANE

"What the hell happened to your ankle?" Owen said, once Dane was seated in the back of the SUV.

"Don't," she said, as Rebecca tried wrapping it as she tried to listen to Nehale on the phone.

Rebecca ignored her.

The conversation with Nehale was apparently for her ears only and yet she was surrounded by her old fire crew from what seemed like another lifetime, long ago. But it was, in reality, only a few weeks ago that they were fighting in Chicago together and then Tuck fell to his death and she killed Cal.

What they didn't know was that she'd killed again since then. Only Matthew knew, but he wasn't aware of the details just yet.

"What happened to our escort car?" Dane said to Nehale.

"He's needed elsewhere at the moment. Your crew has the directions to your next destination, Dane. If you need anything between here and there, we'll be here for you if we can help. You just need to reach out."

"Uh-huh. Is this a good time for you to tell me who's funding this whole endeavor? I was pretty sure this was a personal matter, and no one knew my motives, but something tells me you do know my motives," Dane said.

"I like the way she says 'motives'," Rebecca said.

Dane shot her daggers. And then her daggers softened a little because she was Rebecca and she was in the truck with her and she seemed healthy and well, but still annoying.

"Yes. We're aware of your motives and Ms. Talbot, you must know who's funding this mission. You're a very wealthy woman," Nehale said.

"Wait, what?" Dane said, but the call faded suddenly, and she found herself meeting Matthew's eyes.

"It has to be Paul, Dane. He's got to be alive," Matthew said.

"Alive? But we were sure he wouldn't survive," Dane said.

He shrugged. "Maybe he did."

It was Lee who said, "He could have just left a big trust fund and directions. I mean, he was the Rebel Blaze guy, right? They said he took a modest salary but never spent a dime."

"That's because it wasn't his money to spend. It was Dane's all along," Owen said.

"It was my father's," Dane corrected. "It was his invention." And then, like that night so long ago was just yesterday, she flashed on her father's body lying there in the fire-engulfed room where she once lived, and Paul had to drag her away. It was so wrong how he'd died, and now she knew the whole truth.

But that was then and what happened after that was why she was on this mission now. Jolting herself into action she said, "Lee, we're on the right path? Let's get through town and then we can take turns driving. There's no time to waste. I can't explain," she said to all of them, "but I've got to get to Texas before they release the DNA site."

"We know," Matthew said.

"What do you know?" Dane asked, hoping no one knew.

"We've been informed of the location in Tivoli, Texas, that

you need to get to before they release the information. The question we all have, Dane, is why?" Matthew said with soft brown eyes while he reached for her hand.

She let him weave his fingers between her own but suspected he thought he knew everything about her. He didn't. He didn't know *everything*, and she wanted to keep it that way. She had to protect her secret, just like she had to protect those she'd come to love.

But that also meant Nehale did know her secret or the end goal of her mission would not have been revealed, and that was impossible. There was only one person who knew about Tivoli, Texas, and that was the person holding the secret, although that secret would be revealed in short order, all over the news in the next few days. And she had to get to the secret first.

"I hate to bring this up," Lee's voice interrupted her thoughts. "We have a 36-hour trip ahead of us and this thing will need fuel at a time when gas is hard to come by. Do you think the little man in the phone has any plans? Because I can see the digital needle on this thing has a lifespan and the fuse is lit."

Matthew looked at Dane.

Dane shrugged.

30

MATTHEW

Dane had fallen asleep. He still held her hand even though her fingers were slack and sweaty.

"She wouldn't take anything for the swollen ankle. Are we sure she's okay?" Owen whispered.

"Yep. She's in drive mode. We just need to make sure she eats and sleeps and stay out of her way," Matthew said and looked at the digital map he fingered on the console. "Okay, we turn south at Yakima, people. We've been all over this neck of the woods before. Lee, how much do you still have in you before you need relief?"

"I'm good until Umatilla, I'd say, but we'll need gas before then. That's still an issue. We're on half a tank now," Lee said.

"Yep. I think we call a friend on that one. I mean, we can find gas stations, but will they allow us to simply pull up and take more than our ration?" Owen said.

"Well, there've got to be a few smaller mom and pop places, right?" Rebecca said.

"Are we gas bandits now? No, I don't think so. That's a great way to get shot in the back," Lee said, staring Rebecca down in the rearview mirror.

She giggled.

That's when Matthew's phone lit up again.

"Hello," Matthew said, rolling his eyes.

"Hello Matthew. Our monitors see that you're down to half a tank of gas. Expect a fuel delivery every time this happens."

"Oh. We were just discussing our conversion to gas pirates and ripping off the next mom and pop station that we happened by. When do we pull over?"

Nehale laughed for the first time, and Matthew wasn't sure he liked the sound of it. "No need to pull over. You'll hardly notice the intrusion."

For the second time in the last few moments, Matthew pulled the phone away from his ear and looked at it with a strange fascination. "Intrusion?"

"Yes, and we realize your rations are short. We'll do our best to also drop off water and a few other essentials," Nehale said.

That look again.

"Umm, all right," Matthew said.

"Matthew, how is Ms. Talbot? Does she seem all right to you?" Nehale asked.

"I...no. Her ankle's busted up. She's clearly got a knot on her head and several lacerations. But she barely let anyone help her," Matthew said.

"That's not exactly what I meant. We realize she's getting some much-needed rest at the moment, but we just wanted to know how her state of mind is."

Matthew took a breath and tried to keep his voice even. "Who exactly is *we*? I realize this is likely Paul's doing. What I don't know is if he's alive or dead. If it's the latter, I'd really like to know who *we* is. I have a hard time understanding your motives otherwise."

"Tell him *we* have a hard time understanding his motiv... their motives," Owen said.

Matthew shook his head.

Nehale did that laugh again. "All will be revealed in time. Just know we have the best of intentions for Ms. Talbot and her goals."

Then there was silence, except for the rumble of the road beneath them.

"What the hell is *that*?" Lee said.

Matthew shrugged his shoulders and then looked at Dane sleeping in the backseat. So many questions. Where had she been? What was she up against now? And they were along for the ride.

"That's not what I meant," Lee said. "What the hell is *that*, coming up behind us. Look."

Owen shot up in front of Matthew, blocking his view out the window.

"Is that some kind of storm cloud?" Rebecca said.

"Sort of, darling. It's a drone cloud. And it's coming this way. Get us out of here, Lee!"

They all watched as the dark mass came closer still.

"Faster, Lee!" Rebecca said.

Lee pressed the accelerator down. "We're headed into curves, over the Gorge. I can't go that fast. We'll lose control."

Matthew took the pistol John had given him and rechecked the load. "Six rounds. How good a shot are you, Owen?"

"There's like fifty of those things. We won't make a dent. What the hell do they want?"

That's when Lee let off the gas suddenly. "Guys, I think I know what this is. Calm down."

"What are you doing?" Owen yelled. "Here they come!"

"Trust me...I think we're about to get a delivery," Lee said.

Matthew watched with the pistol in his hand, ready to fire, but as the cloud neared the black mass spread out into a running line and that's when he saw they each held a container.

"Holy mother...that nearly gave me a heart attack," Rebecca said. "Look at that—they're all taking their turn filling the tank."

"We don't have to open anything?" Owen said.

"Must be a rubber bladder. That's pretty cool," Matthew said and then checked the fuel gauge. "We're nearly full."

Lee said, "Can you imagine where that gas came from? We'd be lucky to find a few gallons on our own. Something big is behind this, for sure."

Eyes landed on Dane again as she slept through it all.

Then Matthew was startled by a tap on his passenger window.

Lee swerved a little. "Holy crap, that scared me. We're going fifty and we get a food delivery," he said.

Matthew lowered the window and slipped the bag off a catch latch at the end of the drone's handle. As soon as the drone was alleviated of its burden, it shot up into the air a bit and off it went veering at an angle up into the sky.

"What will they think of next?" Owen said.

"What's in the bag?" Rebecca said.

Matthew opened it and found several bottles of water and with them, several packets of powder.

"The last thing we need at the moment is alcohol," Lee said.

"Not so fast," Owen said. "I'm still shaking from the drone cloud. I could use a hit."

Matthew flipped the packets over in his hand and saw the familiar Rebel Blaze logo but beneath that were the words *Protein Electrolytes, What Every Body Needs.*

"Oh, that's clever marketing. *Every Body.* You know, like everybody!" Rebecca said.

Matthew shook his head and said, "Okay, here. Everyone take one. I think this means we don't actually get food, but these should keep us going so we don't need to stop. Save one for

Dane. No trading. Why are you trading? I thought they were all the same."

"I don't like pineapple," Rebecca said. "See, it says pineapple."

"At least it's not meatloaf," Matthew said.

"Seriously, they have meatloaf flavor?" Lee said.

"Mine says tootie frootie. What the hell is that?" Owen said but no one answered him. "I'll save that one for Dane."

Matthew shot him a look.

"What? Snoozers losers. I'll take the apple one."

Lee said as Matthew mixed his water, "What I don't get is how did they escape the no-fly zone? I thought that meant drones as well."

"They must be flying below the radar," Owen said.

Matthew shook his head while staring out his window over the desert-like terrain of Eastern Washington. "I don't think so. They're somehow evading detection. I watched them fly right up."

"Maybe they have a Faraday cage around them to evade detection," Rebecca said.

"Nah, then they wouldn't have the capability of redirection. There's no way that would work. They need to receive a live signal," Lee said.

"It's got to be something like that, though," Owen said.

And that's when Matthew said, "Oh..." because off in the distance where the drones had disappeared, there was a midair fireball explosion reflecting back on the glass window. "...they're expendable!"

31

DANE

Threads of terror invaded her dreams. As luck would have it, she'd learned to wake herself as a comforting balm. While her nerves settled down, Dane tried to remember where she was, and with one sight of Matthew driving, it all came back to her. Both the good and the bad.

By the looks of it, it was dusk on one end or the other of a day—or many days; she couldn't tell which yet. But on waking to this day, she was happy to watch Matthew's strong profile while he stared at the open road. He was a good man, solid and dependable, and she wished her life could be normal so that she could relinquish her soul to him, but that wasn't going to happen. Instead, he was risking his life for hers against her will, and he had no idea what he was getting himself into—what they were all getting themselves into by associating with her. She had to keep that in mind. She would not drag them through more danger if it came to it; she would find a way to go on her own once again to keep them safe but for now, as a tear slid down her the bridge of her nose, she watched Matthew drive.

He glanced at her in the backseat after a few minutes, obviously feeling her stare. "Hey," he whispered with a tentative glance in the passenger seat.

Dane looked there too and saw someone slumped down in the seat sleeping. It was likely Lee.

"Are you okay?" he asked.

She nodded.

Grabbing a bottle of water, he handed it to her. "Here. Drink this. It's already mixed up."

She reached for it but said, "I...don't need anything to drink."

"It's a food supplement. Compliments of your friend Nehale."

She grasped the bottle and opened the lid. "He's not my friend."

"Well, your employee, I guess is more appropriate."

"I...I don't know what to call him. I have no idea what's really going on here. I'm just trying to get where I'm going."

"Drink up," he said.

A little brighter now, she noticed and pulled the bottle away. "This is really sweet stuff. What's in it?"

Matthew shrugged and shot her a smile. "I really have no idea," then added, "probably nanobots," under his breath.

"You guys stopped somewhere?" she said. "I slept through it all?" She sat up and chugged more of the water.

"Uh, well..." he said, looking down at the fuel level. "You'll find out how we restocked Nehale-style in, I suspect, a few minutes."

She wasn't sure what that meant but looked around at the others sleeping in the SUV. Three more. Three more lives to worry about destroying. She gulped down more of the water.

"Where are we exactly?" she said, staring out at the landscape. There were few trees in the distance. It looked a little like southern Montana, but it wasn't. It was much dryer, with fewer trees. More *scrabby,* if she had to describe it.

"Just passed by Boise. We had to skirt around it a bit, but we made it through without incident. Or at least that's what the map is telling me. What the hell, Dane? I know I'm not supposed to ask questions but what the hell's going on?" he whispered.

She sat in the middle of the seat and sucked down more liquid. "I..." she began to say but something out of the front windshield caught her eye. "Matthew, watch out!" she yelled and dropped her water bottle.

"No, calm down. It's okay," Matthew said, raising one hand, but Dane ducked as a sea of drones were about to collide in a head-on crash.

But nothing happened.

Dane looked up and watched as one after the other lined up beside the SUV as it blazed down the highway at a high rate of speed.

"See?" he said calmly. "No need to worry," he smiled. "Nehale has it all under control. Oh look," he said and rolled down the window as he drove. "A delivery." He cheerfully took a bag from a drone, saying. "Thanks, little buddy. Oh and hey, thanks for your service." The drone shot up into the air after that and Matthew closed the window and then handed her the bag. "Here you go, help yourself."

"What?...what just happened?" Dane said, holding the bag.

Not using the cheerful voice from before, Matthew furrowed his brow at her and said, "That's what I would like to know, Dane. What the hell is this? Who's doing this?"

"When did this start?" she asked, still holding the bag.

"Hours ago and oh, watch out the window for a few seconds...right...about...now," Matthew said.

A light flashed in the sky just after that.

"What?" she said.

Matthew flung his hand out, "They were just blown to smithereens. Happens every half a tank refill."

She opened the bag then and glanced at packets and water bottles. She mumbled while thinking it all through, "You should probably not name them *Little Buddy*, then."

Matthew let out a growl.

Ignoring him, she asked, "How much farther do we have to go?"

"Be my guest and pull up the map," he motioned to the center console.

"I can't reach it," she said.

"You can do it from there on the back of the seat; there's another one. Hell, it activates from the back as well. Go ahead and try. See what I mean?"

Dane held the translucent map out before her and opened her fingers to widen the angle. She wanted to know just exactly where Nehale got his information, and when she opened up the exact destination in Tivoli, she gasped a little. Her heart sank a lot. Hell, you could walk up the virtual porch steps of the little yellow house. The image was so clear even the quarter white wagon wheel spokes were visible in the corners of the screen door that she'd heard slap closed behind her a few years ago. Dread instantly flooded her veins. Closing the map quickly she said, "How do I find the news on this thing?" flashing through virtual buttons.

"Hold on, hold on," Matthew said loud enough to make Lee stir in his seat. "What's wrong, Dane?"

She flashed a glance in his eyes in the rearview mirror. He was watching her.

"Nothing," she said, ignoring him. Then she found what she was looking for and what Nehale said was true. They were releasing the information sooner than she'd hoped. She flashed from one news headline to the next. It was inevitable. The secret was soon to be revealed. But the question was, who was watching? No one, she hoped, but she couldn't take that chance. She wasn't sure if Bill had told anyone or if he even knew.

"Dane," Matthew said, "how are you feeling?"

"I'm fine."

"Liar," he said.

"Look, can we not do this, please?" Dane said, and she could tell Matthew was about to say something, but Owen said it for her from the third row seat.

"Yeah. Some of us are trying to sleep, Matthew," Owen said.

"It's your turn to drive soon, Owen," Matthew said. "You might as well wake up."

"Did the delivery come again?" Owen asked.

"Yes," Matthew said.

"Well, the problem is...we've got to stop anyway...just for a minute or two, if you get my meaning. Unless there's a drone for that too...which I'll pass, if that's the case."

They all started laughing at that but even Dane took a suspicious peek out the window just to make sure.

"All right, I see a cluster of trees ahead. I'll pull over for a brief minute and then everyone out. Do your business and then get back in. Girls first," Matthew said, and Dane was not about to argue with him.

32

MATTHEW

After they pulled over for a much-needed break, Owen settled behind the wheel and Matthew slid into the seat next to Dane. "All right. We're a third of the way there, more or less," Matthew said. "Do we need equipment before we get there? Is there something we need to gear up for or do you have that covered with Nehale?"

She looked at him with a raised eyebrow. "What are you talking about? Gear up for what exactly?"

"I..." he shook his head at her. "That's what I mean, Dane. We don't have a clue what we're diving into here. Can you at least tell us something?"

He watched her unscrew the water bottle cap and pour the contents of one of the packets through the mouth. She was avoiding the conversation like all get out.

"I told you that I could do this on my own. I didn't ask for you, or anyone else, to come along," she said evenly.

He knew that was true. He knew she'd gladly walk away like she'd always done before to take on the monster or whatever the hell it was that she was fighting all on her own, but the problem was...that he didn't want her to do it all on her own. He cared about her. He'd go as far as to admit to himself that he loved her, desperately. But she didn't need to know that. It would only complicate things.

"Just stop. We're here with you and that's all there is to it. Get used to it. Keep an eye on Owen and wake me if anything else happens. And don't name the drones," he added, and Owen nodded.

"Drones go kaboom," Owen said under his breath.

Matthew smiled and shook his head and then drifted off to sleep.

WHAT SEEMED LIKE MOMENTS LATER, he woke to the sounds of screaming.

33

DANE

"My gods, how do you sleep with that guy?" Rebecca said, staring at Dane. "It's going on ten hours. His snoring would drive me insane. It already is; I've lost my mind," she said covering her ears.

Dane wasn't sure what to say about that. She was still stunned that Rebecca found her too familiar with Matthew's snoring. In actuality she found the cadence somehow comforting while she researched the news for relevant information. She'd even taken a nap during that time and rewrapped her ankle.

"Can you just keep your hands on the steering wheel?" Lee said. "You're making me nervous. Who let you drive anyway?"

"Hey man, I can drive," Rebecca said.

"Hey...man," Owen said in a lower tone.

Dane rolled her eyes.

"Oooh, big man mad," Rebecca said.

Dane flipped off the screen because she'd been waiting for something and just as predicted, she glanced again at the fuel gauge and then through the window again. The dark cloud approached right on schedule.

"It's drone time," Rebecca announced, and Dane rolled down her window.

"What are you doing?" Lee asked.

But before she answered, she reached her arm out underneath the whirling blade and grabbed one of the drones above the fuel container as it lined up behind its brothers.

"Dane, what the hell are you doing? Don't!" Owen yelled.

Rebeca screamed.

Lee yelled, "Watch the road, woman!"

Matthew sat up.

The drone tried readjusting as she held it slightly out of its desired path. The other drones bobbed up and down and readjusted in front of the derelict one and when she released it, the other drones parted and let him in line again.

"Aww," Rebecca said.

"That's weird," Owen said and released his hold on Dane's shoulders. "Let me try," he said.

She looked at Matthew, who hadn't said a word but looked as if he could chew nails.

Despite that she said, "What if we pulled one inside the truck?"

"Aww," Rebecca repeated. "We could save them."

"It's not a pet, Dane," Owen said.

"I'm not..." She looked at Owen like he was nuts. "I'm not trying to make a pet out of them. I..."

"She's trying to say we could use them. We could maybe even reprogram one. For what, Dane?" Lee said.

"She means a bomb," Matthew said.

"Ooh," Rebecca said, her voice solemn, "so not a pet then."

Ignoring her, Dane said, "Except that I don't know how to reprogram them."

"Lee does," Matthew said. "Don't you?"

"Yes. Yes, I do. We used drones in my last unit. It might be possible with the fancy phones you've got there." Then Lee rolled down his window and accepted the latest hydration packs from the delivery drone. "I think it's time we pulled over for a minute," Lee said.

"Why? I don't have to go yet," Rebecca said.

"Yes, you do," Lee said.

34

MATTHEW

It was the first sleep any of them had in several tense days and even though it was in rotation, they were all grateful. Although being reunited with Dane wasn't what he'd hoped...it was what he expected, just not what he had foolishly hoped, he told himself. The drone idea bothered him but intrigued him at the same time. Dane's idea told him she was still in fight mode, not survival mode, which was good but still not where he wanted to be with her in life. If they could just get through this, if he could just help her solve her problem then maybe...maybe they'd have a future together. Or was he fooling himself again? Maybe in this world, that's all there was. One tragic problem after another one.

"Okay, here they come," Owen said. "Who's going to do the deed?"

"I'm doing it," Dane said. "If there's a problem, I don't want the rest of you dealing with it. Just focus on driving," she said, as she reached for the fifth one in line, blades whirring.

"Can you...how do you turn off their motors?" Rebecca said.

"Hand me a jacket," Dane said.

"You'll burn the motor out," Matthew warned.

"Let me do it," Lee said and opened his own window. He looked at Dane. "Listen, hold him still. Rebecca, you toss the jacket over the blades and I'll turn him off, then Dane pulls him inside. Understand?" They all nodded.

"That's a lot of fuel you're bringing on board," Matthew said. "I'll make room to set him down."

And like an assembly line, Dane looped her fingers around the neck above the fuel container and below the whirring blades and pulled it closer to the window, where Rebecca covered the blades temporarily with her light jacket and Lee quickly reached for the engine near the blades and switched a little black knob in the other direction.

"Rebecca, take the jacket off," Lee said.

"Oh, that's my part too," she said.

Then Dane brought the drone inside the window carefully, so as not to knock the fuel tank, and handed it to Matthew. She then reached out and grabbed another one.

"So how many?" Rebecca asked.

"Let's start with three and see what happens," Matthew said.

"Okay, but that's three loads of fuel we don't have to run on. Don't forget that," Owen said.

"Yes, but I've got a feeling they calculate on an expendable percentage. I bet they send a few extra next time," Matthew said. "Knowing a few of these guys don't actually make their final destination."

Dane handed him the final drone.

"Yay, teamwork," Rebecca said and tried to high-five Dane.

She just smiled.

"Except that my hands smell like gas now," Rebecca said.

"Yeah, there is that. Actually the whole cabin smells like gas. Open the windows," Matthew said.

"No worries," Lee said as he grabbed a screwdriver from the compartment toolbox. I don't think this will take too long to test." Opening a panel on the drone he said, "Let's see what we have here. Okay, so, the idea is to switch this to operation two instead of hijacking program one, which might alert our friends. Let me see your phone, Dane. Thanks, then if we open the program app..."

"Jeez, man. I had no idea you knew *this* much about drones," Matthew said.

"I'm making it up as I go," Lee said without looking up.

"My eyes are watering," Rebecca said, fanning her face with her hands.

"Yeah, the fumes are rough," Matthew said. "If this works, we can try store them on the roof."

"What are we going to use them for?" Rebecca said.

And that's when they all stared at one another, and then at Dane.

"Why let a good bomb go to waste? Always be prepared," she said.

Still no answers, Matthew thought.

"Okay." The drone's blades lifted slowly and then let down again. "It's under my command. Let's try this," Lee said.

Matthew picked it up and handed it to Dane. She held it out the window and lifted it up above her head. Then they watched as it unfolded its blades and took off. It was a moment for Matthew, though. He wasn't watching the drone. He was watching Dane. Her hair flying in the wind. The look of wonder on her face. It was a moment. A snapshot of her not worried about a thing, the briefest seconds of time with not a worry in the world. No vengeance, no pain, just...wonder. And then she reached back inside the cab and grabbed the shotgun and aimed it at the drone.

"Now!" yelled Lee, and the explosion was a bright burst in a darkening sky.

35

DANE

"It's Rebecca's turn to sleep, thank the gods," Lee said as Dane drove. He took a swig of his bottle of water.

"Why does she annoy you so much?" Dane asked, watching as a semi-truck passed them in the opposite lane.

"She doesn't annoy me, really. She just reminds me of my little sister," Lee said, and a goofy grin spread out over his face and then disappeared just as suddenly.

Something happened there. Dane wasn't going to ask. Some things you know about another in the briefest of seconds and you make the decision to open the wound or not. There was no point in opening that wound. His troubles were his own. And she only had the time and bandwidth for her own.

One white lane after the other slipped under the wheels and Dane was fine with the silence as they neared her goal.

"We'll be there in the next five hours. Owen heard the Texas border is closed. How do you think we'll get across?" Lee asked.

She let her eyes roll to the top of her head in answer.

"Blast your way through? I hope our friend Nehale has a subtler approach," Lee said.

"Yes, I agree," she nodded. "That's what he said anyway. They're working on a crossing."

"They've got to know we have twenty of those drones strapped to the roof of this truck," Matthew said from the back seat. "I'm surprised they haven't said anything yet. They're probably listening to us now."

Dane shrugged her shoulders. She didn't care who was listening, as long as she was closing the distance. Then the screen opened up on the console revealing their new friend, Nehale.

"Hello there. It's like you know we're talking about you," she said.

He smiled and nodded.

"But you look like crap," Matthew said. "Have you even slept? We've been taking shifts."

Nehale smiled and nodded again. "You've been quite busy, I hear. Ingenious even."

"Uh, thank you," Matthew said, and Dane thought the compliment seemed genuine.

"We're a diverse group," Matthew said.

"Yes and that's good because as you were stating, the Texas border is blocked. We've been working on a diplomatic way of trying to get you through and oddly enough, we think we've found one," Nehale said. "As you've heard, they've declared their sovereignty and after poring through their newly posted declaration we think we've found a less than lethal way of storming the border."

"Oh darn, we were hoping to put the drone bombs to good use," Owen said.

Matthew cleared his throat. "Let's not piss off the Texans if we can keep from it. Since they have a history with mosquitos, something tells me they won't have a problem with drone bombs."

"We need a catchier name for those," Owen said.

"Shh," Dane said because Nehale was trying to say something.

"Well, Mr. Owen Johnson," Nehale said.

"Here," Owen said.

"You were born in Texas?" Nehale asked.

"Yes, that's right. How'd you know?" Owen said.

"We've run background checks on all of Ms. Talbot's associates," Nehale said, "and that's a good thing because since you are from Texas originally, you have a passport through the border with your birth certificate that's associated with your driver's license."

"But my license is from Montana," Owen said.

"Not anymore. Any and all licenses are now nationalized. Things in Washington are changing rapidly. We know it's hard to keep up. We are sending you a new birth certificate in the next drone delivery in case they don't accept that one, since they are no longer a part of the United States."

"Man, that means we're breaking into another country. Not a state," Owen said.

Matthew said, "Wait, that means you have dual citizenship?"

They all looked at Nehale for the answer.

"At this very moment in time, yes, but watch your newsfeed for further updates. With a citizen on board, we are hoping they will let the rest of you through as well. Since you are his guests. Understand?"

"Ah...you're my guests," Owen said. "Only I can get you through."

Dane had to smile at the irony.

Nehale wasn't finished. "In all seriousness, they do not have a sense of humor at the moment. The stories are grim. But you can't blame them; they've lost more than most in the last few years."

And that news made Dane's stomach clench and her foot pressed the accelerator just a little bit more. She'd stowed her secret there long ago.

"Nehale," she said, "what about the database? The clock's ticking. Is there any indication of what we discussed privately?"

Nehale's eyes flashed amongst them. He looked a little confused, or was that annoyance? She wasn't sure.

"Yes, the clock is ticking and yes, our suspicion has evidence behind it now. There is a direct correlation with your hypothesis."

"What the hell did you just say?" Matthew looked from the screen to Dane. "What is he talking about?"

"Not now, Matthew," Dane said.

"Ms. Talbot, If I may, your friend has a rig..." but Dane turned off the screen before Nehale could finish what he was about to say.

"Hmm," Lee said, letting out an uncomfortable breath. He then totally avoided the tension hanging in the air between Matthew and Dane and turned to Owen. "That blows. Dual citizenship though, dude, that's cool. So you're from Texas?"

Owen lightly said, "Yeah...yee-haw!"

"You totally don't have an accent though," Lee said.

Dane locked eyes with Matthew through the rearview mirror. Matthew's eyes said he wasn't too pleased with her at the moment. She didn't blame him, but she also could not help him.

Owen said, "Yeah, I've never had one really. My parents split up soon after my birth and I went with my mom to Montana."

"That answers a lot," Lee said with a chuckle.

"What?" Owen said.

36

MATTHEW

I t may well have been the edge of a cliff. A theoretical one at least, but they were all going over it in the next few minutes. And no one seemed to have the least sign of hesitation on their face as he scanned them in the rearview mirror. That was a good thing at least.

The map had them switch from Highway 285 to 380, and it was a straight shot to the border, where the traffic thickened. They hadn't seen this for a while, since they avoided populated areas as much as possible. He checked the map again in case Nehale had them redirected. "Are you ready for this?" he said and looked over to Dane sitting in the passenger seat.

"Yes," she nodded but didn't look back at him. She just stared out the window finger combing her hair in long strands out the window, the sunlight reflecting off the red highlights.

"Are we in line?" Lee said.

"Sort of looks that way," Matthew said and leaned out the driver's window to see if there was something blocking their way. They were a few miles from the border crossing. "It couldn't be backed up this far, could it?"

"Well, we could send a drone bomb to check it out, but I

think that would blow our cover," Owen said.

Lee looked at him. "We don't need cover. We have you, man."

"Oh, yeah," Owen said, holding up his birth certificate.

"And why are we going to your hometown of Tivoli?" Lee asked.

"Because Rebecca and I are getting married and you're the wedding party," Owen said.

Rebecca squealed.

Matthew wasn't sure if Rebecca was aware that they weren't really getting married. It was hard to tell with her sometimes, but he would let Owen deal with that one.

"Okay, we moved another inch. Should we call the man in the little box?" Lee said.

"I'm sure they're working on it," Dane said, and it was the first time she'd spoken in the last few hours.

From the glow of the backseat, he could tell Lee was hovering over the map. "Man, Tivoli should be the heart of Texas. We have to cross the border still and get all the way down there?"

"We just drove across the entire United States and you're just now complaining?" Rebecca said.

"Release the drones," Owen said and leaned forward to Lee and asked, "Could we program them to take off in unison like that...on voice command?"

Lee paused. "No," he said, and shook his head.

Matthew slapped a hand to his forehead and rubbed it down his face. "We've been cooped up together too long."

"Look," Dane said.

Matthew peeked through his fingers out the windshield. "No way. Where did he come from?"

Nehale appeared on the screen suddenly and looked in even worse condition than before.

"Follow the lead car," he said without further explanation.

Matthew was wedged in line but put it in reverse, and then they heard an explosion and saw a fireball engulf several cars ahead of them.

"Go!" Dane yelled.

Despite ramming the car behind them, Matthew revved the engine and pulled out of line, crossing the grassy barrier, and caught up to the black Challenger as it sped down the road.

Dane looked behind them. "What's going on back there?"

"I can't tell," Rebecca said. "Just lots of fire. Hurry, there's a lot of people coming this way."

A red sports car raced past them and nearly rammed the Challenger.

"Are you serious?" Matthew yelled.

"Keep up with the lead car," Nehale said.

"I'm trying, dammit. What the hell happened back there?" Matthew asked. "I thought you guys were keeping an eye on things ahead of us."

"We cannot account for every scenario, unfortunately," Nehale said.

They were speeding down a side road when suddenly the Challenger veered sharp right, going north. "You've got to be kidding me—ahhhh," Matthew said as he grasped the steering wheel and slammed the brakes into action in a turn that should have rolled them over.

"Oh, wait. We lost a drone," Rebecca yelled.

Matthew looked out the window and saw it tumbling down the highway end over end and then burst into an explosion about the size of a Volkswagen.

"Aww," she gasped.

"He's up ahead there," Dane said, pointing.

"They're shooting now," Lee said.

"Who's shooting? At us? Where's it coming from?" Matthew said.

That's when Dane suddenly came to life and began shooting off orders. "Matthew, don't worry about anything but keeping up with that car."

"Lee, get the drones ready if we need them." Then she picked up the rifle and tossed it to Owen. "Out the window," she said, with a tilt of her head. "Rebecca, grab a drone front to rooftop and fling it behind us if needed.

She nodded repeatedly but didn't seem too sure. "Uhh, okay."

"Keep your heads down." Then Dane sat down again and looked at the screen. "You're doing fine, Matthew."

He nodded and could not believe where she'd gone before, but was grateful she'd come back to him now.

"Nehale, I need you to tell me where we're going now."

"I don't know yet," Nehale said. "I'm working on it. We're looking ahead for a clearing."

"Why is that?"

"We haven't figured it out yet, quite honestly."

She nodded. Something was going on. She'd figured something out, but she still wasn't sharing it with him.

"Lee," she said, "send the drone over to the lead car."

"What are you doing?" Matthew said.

They all started talking at once.

"Do it now, Lee," Dane said and grabbed the pistol.

Nehale disappeared from the screen.

The Challenger skidded to a stop on the dirty side of the road, sending dust flying. Other cars whizzed past them.

"Pull over, Matthew," Dane said.

He wasn't sure he should, but he followed her lead.

Dane opened the door.

"What about the drone? I've got one up," Lee asked as she stepped out of the truck and held the pistol down.

She looked back at them and said, "Hover."

37

DANE

The suspicion was driving her nuts. She had to know it was him and not Mathus, somehow. And she had to know now. She hoped like hell she was right, but if she was wrong...there'd be hell to pay. And if she was wrong, she couldn't lead an enemy into Texas and right to her goal. *What if it's her? What if she already knows and I'm leading her right in?* The senator would have inside knowledge since she backed the DNA Release Initiative, and it wasn't as if she had any problem using her extensive resources, no matter how unethical they might be, to achieve her goals. But did she even know? That was the question.

Despite it all, she knew whoever was in that car would not shoot her. She was valuable to them, either for their greed or for their grief. So she stepped over the dry New Mexico ground, tawny dust flying in knee high puffs with each step until she was halfway there. Hearing a light buzz, she took her eyes off the glaring blacked out windshield of the Challenger and spotted the drone bomb hovering about ten feet above the hood. She was about to tell Lee to back off a little when the door of the

Challenger opened up with a click and a long jeaned leg with a white Adidas attached pushed open the rest.

Could it really be him? Was he alive after all?

A hand clenched the side of the door and the man within stepped out with his back to her.

He turned and took one look at her before she lowered her weapon and bolted into him.

"How dare you!"

38

MATTHEW

"I knew it was him all along," Owen said.

They were all glued to the scene unfolding before them.

"You don't...you don't even know his name," Matthew said.

"Yeah, I do...it's that Paul guy. The one that's dead," Owen said.

Rebecca said, "Well, clearly, he is not dead."

"He is going to be dead in a few minutes if she keeps shoving him like that," Lee pointed out.

"Hey, you guys stay right here," Matthew said, with a click of the door as he tilted his head. "And Lee, you might wanna take the drone back a few feet, in case..."

"In case she explodes it with her mind. Man, she's pissed. Look at her face," Owen said.

Rebecca hit him. "She's not pissed. She's so happy, she's crying. See?"

"*That* means she's happy?" Owen said, pointing at her. "No seriously...how can that expression be happy? I'm trying to learn."

Matthew slammed the door shut and focused on Dane and Paul instead.

They saw him coming so he took his time with long, slow steps and saw that the drone seemed to retreat as if it were disappointed it didn't get to explode itself.

"...you let us believe you were dead!"

Yeah, that didn't look like happiness to Matthew. That sounded like she wanted to claw his eyes out.

She had hold of Paul's shirt with one hand and a pistol in the other. That wasn't a good idea. Not if you wanted to keep someone alive. Being pissed is one thing. Stupid is something else. And Dane wasn't stupid, she was just dealing with a storm of emotions she wasn't equipped to handle. He imagined it was something like relief or gratitude. Those were two emotions Dane didn't tangle with often. It was probably a lot for her at the moment. That's what he was thinking as he walked up behind her and took the pistol from her right hand.

Despite the yelling. Paul nodded at him in a gesture that meant hello.

Matthew nodded back and noted that Paul was in fact alive but looked as if he'd been chewed up by some bad drugs.

"I think we ought to calm this down a notch, Dane. We need to get over the border before nightfall and I'm pretty sure this is not the way to avoid detection."

"Paul," Matthew nodded at him again. "Glad you're alive."

"Thanks," he said.

"Why didn't you tell me? We thought you were dead! Why hide behind your assistant?" Dane yelled again.

Paul did his best to remain calm. He grabbed her wrists and looked into her eyes. "I nearly died, Dane. I wanted to die for years, after what I did to you and your father. You two were the only things I ever cared about."

Matthew cleared his throat, stood a couple feet away and scanned the horizon in all directions, but listened all the same.

"And then Kim," he shook his head. "It was all my fault. I'm just trying to make it right. I have spent *years* trying to make this right. And then *your daughter*, Dane...I'm so sorry that happened to you."

Matthew blurted out, "Whhhat?" with a jerk of his head.

Paul glanced at him but they both ignored the question.

And that's how Matthew found out Dane had a daughter. This was all for her somehow....and then he pieced all the fuzzy broken ends of the vague puzzle together, where they locked into a new, elusive picture. Now he somewhat understood. Now the vengeance might be justified. Now the urgency over the DNA kind of seemed related, and the clock was ticking on that, but why?

"How did you know?" Dane cried, tears flowing down her face.

Paul shook his head. "I knew he was a bad guy, Dane. I'd heard the stories going through campus, and he had a powerful mother. We know how powerful she is now. She's great at hiding things. Hiding people. And if she knows about this...

"Your actions after... The prolonged disappearance after Daniel's death. I'd been tracking you for years, but I didn't realize what exactly had happened until recently, and then I backtracked your steps. Dane, you've been carrying this inside you all this time. Not only did you lose your father that night, you lost so much more. And I was a part of that destruction and I'm so damn sorry."

Matthew was stunned but now both Dane and Paul were sobbing and there were suddenly sirens coming from some-where. He hoped they weren't for them.

Dane looked at him for the first time.

"We've got to go," Matthew said and pulled Dane's arm gently away.

Paul wiped his eyes and gave a sharp nod. "Follow me then. There's another path to the border. Dane," Paul said, and she stopped in her tracks and turned back. "Don't worry. We'll get to her before they do, Dane. I promise you. We'll have her before they find out."

Dane stopped in her tracks. "How much do you know?"

Matthew tugged her away then and wondered where they all stood after all this, and where they might be going and hell, he hated himself for thinking it then, but was she *his* or was she *Paul's?* Because she couldn't be both.

39

DANE

Dane slipped into the passenger seat and Matthew closed the door without meeting her eyes.

She flung one sleeved arm over her left eye and then the other, and it was so quiet in the cab as Matthew walked around the front of the truck, she turned to see if the others were still in the back or if they'd escaped the madness and ran in the other direction, away from her crazy life.

Their side eyes met hers, though, as they sat silently looking as if they were afraid to move.

Matthew opened the door and got behind the wheel and still, no one spoke as he turned on the engine and followed Paul.

Finally, "Drone back in place?" Matthew said.

"Yeah," Lee said.

Why would Paul hide himself from them? That was the one thing she couldn't understand yet. Why the mystery? To know he survived the shooting was a miracle. He'd lost so much blood that night he took the bullet meant for her, they never thought he'd make it after saving her life. It should have been her who died that day.

She shook her head and glanced at the road ahead of them as the lead car rambled on down the narrow road.

"He did it for you, Dane. Don't you see that?" Matthew said quietly.

She looked at him crossly. She didn't want to talk about it in front of the others, even though she knew they had a lot to talk about.

"He..." she shook her head. "He should have at least reached out to let us know he was alive."

"Yeah," Matthew said. "There're a lot of things people should do or should say...but they have their reasons for keeping things to themselves. Can you tell me her name?"

Dane shook her head and huffed a little. What he said was true and she understood his frustration with her, but she was clear that she had things to take of that didn't involve him or anyone else.

Then they watched as Paul took another sharp right turn at a four-way intersection and Nehale appeared on the screen almost simultaneously.

"I swear, he's doing that on purpose. Tell him we need a little more warning before he takes a corner," Matthew complained as he tried to make the turn.

"Hi Nehale. Tell me we're headed to an easy border crossing. This day's been stressful enough," Dane said to the man on the screen.

Nehale looked tired but happier than he did before, and he nodded. "Yes, you are headed there now. I've secured the route for Paul and he's leading you there."

"Why didn't you tell us it was Paul driving the car?"

"I had my orders, Ms. Talbot."

Matthew barked, "Technically, don't you work for her?"

Nehale swallowed. "You'll be there shortly. Please have Owen sit up front and handle the paperwork directly with border security."

"Should we hide the weapons?" Rebecca said, holding up the shotgun.

"No ma'am. This is Texas we're talking about. Lay them out in the open," Nehale said.

"Ooh," Rebecca said.

Though Dane knew she really didn't know.

The brake lights ahead of her told them they were now in line, and Dane scooted to the middle row of seats and made way for Owen to clamber up front.

"This is going to be fun!" Owen said.

"Don't get too excited," Matthew said.

"We're getting married!" Rebecca shouted.

Dane widened her eyes and shook her head while she took the seat behind Matthew's.

"So I'm the Texan. How's he getting into the country? He's not invited to the wedding," Owen said, pointing at Paul's car.

Nehale answered before Dane or Matthew could. "He has his own documentation to enter."

"Is it legit, like mine?" Owen asked.

Nehale ignored the question. "Let's concentrate on the border crossing, please."

"Okay, we're nearly there," Matthew said.

"Yes, I'm aware," Nehale said as he typed some keys and Dane watched him, assuming he was in the United States somewhere monitoring every move they made. The glow of a monitor reflected in a tiny distorted rectangle from the whites of Nehal's eyes.

As if he felt her stare, he looked up and met her eyes as she sat in the back seat. She turned away while he stretched his neck one way and then the other. They must be getting close and

Nehale had his doubts this would work because Dane always regarded that tell as a sign of gearing up for imminent battle, just as she anticipated a jump into a fire.

"Owen," Nehale said, "take a deep breath. I'll be right here monitoring the situation, but the screen will go dark. Understand?"

"Yeah man, but what are you going to do if it doesn't work?"

"Always have a plan B my friend," Nehale said and the screen blanked out to a charcoal gray.

"Look. Paul's about to go through," Matthew said.

Owen let out a held breath as Paul's hand appeared through the driver's side window and someone in the booth handed a black ray gun out to scan something.

"Wait, what's he doing? Do we have one of those?" Owen asked.

"Calm down. We're doing it the old-fashioned way, apparently," Matthew said.

"Meaning we're bullshitting our way through," Lee said and they all chuckled while Paul's brake lights went from red to nothing. He pulled forward and Dane watched as he slowly accelerated and then pulled over to the side of a single road along with several other vehicles. Apparently, they were making him get out of his car where officers with dogs were at the ready and sniffing around.

"This is tense. Look what they're doing to Paul," Owen said.

"Shh," Dane said. "We're next."

"Here we go," Rebecca said, low and excited, as if they were about to roll down on a rollercoaster.

"Howdy folks," the border officer said. "What do we have here?"

"A wedding party, sir," Matthew said as Owen handed him his birth certificate and Matthew handed it to the officer.

"So who's getting married?" the officer said.

"We are," Rebecca said with a giggle.

"That would be me and my bride, back there, officer," Owen said, pointing to Rebecca.

The officer craned his neck into the vehicle, taking a look at each and every one of them.

"And who are the rest of these people, Owen Johnson?"

"They're the wedding party, sir. This here is my best man, Matthew Brogen..." Owen said and the officer interrupted the introductions and said, "IDs, please."

Dane fished hers out of her pocket, as everyone else did, but kept an eye on the officer as his brow furrowed over Owen's birth certificate.

Matthew collected the cards and handed them through the window to the officer.

He took them and fanned them out on the surface in front of him. "Mr. Brogen, go ahead and turn off your engine. This may take a while," he said and used his black wand to scan one of the driver's licenses, then looked that the screen and then repeated the process with the rest of them, pulling one of the licenses to the side.

Dane tore her attention away from the process and took a look at Paul, who was still standing beside his car as the officers took a K9 to each wheel well, but otherwise it looked uneventful.

"Your destination," the man in the booth finally said.

"Oh, Tivoli, sir. My parents live nearby. That's where we're having the ceremony," Owen said and nearly sounded convincing.

"And how long do you intend to stay?" the officer asked.

"Four days, sir. Then we're headed back to Montana," Owen said as per the script.

"So you don't plan to reside here?" The officer eyed Owen.

"Ah," Owen faltered.

Damn, no one gave him an answer for that contingency. Dane's palms sweated rivers.

"I....my job is currently keeping me in Montana, sir. I do eventually plan to return home with my bride here."

Good enough, Dane thought and found herself slightly nodding without meaning to.

The officer lifted and lowered his chin.

"All right. It sounds like you're all here for the right reasons. One last question. Is anyone pregnant?" The officer looked directly at Dane. She shook her head and looked down.

"Yes!" Rebecca yelled delightedly.

Dane jerked her head around quickly.

"What?" Owen said.

She smiled. "Well, that's right, honey. I was going to tell you, but I guess you know now."

The officer swept up the IDs and held them tight against the birth certificate and handed them back through the window to Matthew.

"Access denied," the officer said.

"Whaaat?" they all said in unison.

"At this moment in time, we are denying entry to any foreign visitors who are pregnant."

"But I'm a citizen!"

The officer shook his head. "*You*...are welcome. Come right in. But everyone else, including your unborn child, will have to apply for entry, which currently takes four to six weeks."

"That's bul..."

"I would highly advise against any verbal assaults," the officer said.

Matthew placed a hand on Owen's shoulder, but he should have been trying to restrain Dane.

"Up to you, sir. Do you want to enter, or would you like to remain with your friends?"

"I'll pass," Owen seethed.

The officer nodded as Matthew went ahead and turned on the engine and rolled up the window before Owen could say anything else.

"I can't believe that just happened," Lee said.

Dane looked out the window at Paul, who watched them turn away around the little building, and another heavily armed officer waved them past a few bright orange cones, ushering them around and back the way they came.

"I'm so sorry, Dane," Rebecca wailed.

"Why did you say you were pregnant?" Lee yelled.

She cried and held her head in her hands.

"Leave her alone," Owen said.

Dane continued to watch Paul pull his phone from his pocket, accept a paper from the guard and get into the vehicle as they drove on.

"Why? Did you think lying would get us in?" Lee asked more calmly.

"I *am* pregnant," Rebecca yelled with tears rolling down her face. "I didn't think lying about it was a good idea."

"What?" Lee said shaking his head, and Dane noticed Matthew looked at the scene from the rearview mirror, shaking his head.

"Well, that is a new development," Matthew said. "Did you know, Owen?"

"I...you're pregnant?" Owen said, looking stunned for the first time.

From the far backseat, Rebecca smiled through her tears and nodded. "Hmm-uh."

"That's great, baby. I didn't know," Owen said. "We don't have to go to Texas to get married."

"I don't know what in the hell just happened here," Lee said, wiping his brow. "How are we going to get in now?" Lee said, looking at her.

Matthew continued to drive. She knew he didn't have the answers.

Dane shook her head. "I'm sure Nehale's working on it. Can we pull over somewhere? I need a break."

40

MATTHEW

Rebecca's crying was driving him crazy, but more so, Dane's silence. The wheels were turning. Her head down and leaned to the side, he couldn't see her expression from his position. It didn't matter. He knew what she was doing. She'd turned inside herself again. Where she always escaped, alone before, and without him or anyone else.

Maybe she'd let Paul in?

That thought bothered him. He couldn't help but have a bitter taste in his mouth.

Spotting a roadside turn-off with bathrooms nearby, Matthew began to turn and maneuver in line with the rest of those denied entry into the great state—make that country—of Texas.

"What in the bloody hell was that?" Matthew said and surprised himself. "We did everything Nehale said to do. Where is he, anyway?"

"Calm down, man," Owen said.

"I'm so sorry," Rebecca said and a fresh wave of wails began again.

"It's....it's not your fault, Rebecca."

"Hey, man. I'm gonna be a daddy," Owen said as if it just dawned on him.

Matthew nodded. "Yes, congratulations. I just wish we'd known that little piece of information beforehand."

"No one asked me!" Rebecca wailed.

"Is she going to be like this the whole time now?" Lee said, clearly as frustrated as the rest of them.

Matthew pulled into a parking space and Lee was the first one who bolted from the vehicle, pulling at his light t-shirt and heading into the concrete building.

"Why's he so pissed?" Owen said,

Matthew let out a rushed breath. "We're all a bit frustrated." And Matthew began tapping the screen in front of him. "Where the hell *is* he? Dane, can you try to reach our wizard on your phone? He's unresponsive here. Dane?"

Owen jutted his chin out. "She left when Lee did. Went into the bathroom.

Something inside Matthew ticked. "You...watched her walk into the building? You watched her go in?"

"Yeah, she walked right in there. Rebecca followed her."

Matthew felt his muscles relax a little and he slumped into the seat and rubbed his face. "I didn't hear her door open."

"Yeah, she's quiet that way. Too quiet. It's funny. She should be yelling and screaming right now. This seems really important to her but she's a steely one. No reaction at all. That's just not right."

"Oh, but wailing nonstop for the last mile is an acceptable behavior in a closed vehicle with four other individuals present?"

"It's not a competition, man. Settle down. I'll go and relieve myself and you can wait for the little man in the box and then I'll come back and relieve you."

Matthew grabbed the steering wheel and pulled himself up

and away from the seat and realized his t-shirt was sticking to the sweat on his back. Damn, it was hot.

He eyed the women's bathroom doorway. And then Lee came back to the truck.

"Hey man," he said and climbed into the passenger side. "Owen said he wanted to talk to Rebecca in the back."

"Ah," Matthew said. "I don't care who sits next to me."

"As long as it's not Rebecca," they both said under their breaths at the same time and then chuckled.

Nehale appeared on the screen then.

"Hey," Matthew said. "So what's the deal? Where's Paul?"

Nehale smiled and nodded his head as if everything was calm in the world, and Matthew wanted to reach through the little screen and grab the little man around his thin neck and strangle him.

"Paul's standing by and awaiting your response," Nehale said.

"My response? Do you mean Dane's response?" Matthew said.

"I meant collectively, of course," Nehale said.

Matthew glanced at the bathroom door and saw Rebecca some out. Owen had been waiting for her and pulled her into his arms. Matthew glanced down back at the screen to give them a moment to themselves.

"So what's the plan? Is there another way in? Or do we just storm the border? Because I really don't think that's a good idea," Matthew said.

"No, no, that is not a viable solution," Nehale said. "Is Ms. Talbot there? I don't quite see her amongst the rest of you."

Matthew looked up and Rebecca was walking to the truck holding onto Owen's arm.

"Nah, she's in the restroom. She should be out shortly,"

Matthew said and then glanced at Rebecca again and then at the opened bathroom doorway.

"Owen, did you see Dane?" Matthew said when he opened the door.

"No. You saw her in the bathroom?" Owen asked Rebecca.

But Matthew already knew to answer to that question.

41

DANE

They'd wheeled her in. The tiles on the ceiling were pocked and dented. "You're sure you're all right, honey?" the nurse said in a high-pitched honey-sweet voice, her blond hair and ruby red lipstick only fitting for a Texas nurse. No one else could pull that off in a hospital.

Dane nodded.

"You're sure a quiet one. I can see the contractions are comin' on hard. You're in the middle of a big roller coaster now. And you're not even huffin'. That's called *control*. You should hear some of these ladies who come in here. You'd think we were torturing them. All right then, wait right here a quick spell and the doctor will be right in. We'll get the rest of the crew going."

Moments later, "You'll be all right. Hold onto my hand. Push. That's it. Breathe. Don't forget to breathe. Danielle, you're almost there."

A baby wailed then.

"You did it! See there, and she's a dumplin' of a thing."

Dane relaxed into the bed. Her body slumped into the sweaty sheets as if she'd just finished a long run, despite the sting and tugging of the needle and thread below. She turned her head to the side and as the baby wailed, she closed her eyes and listened to the life she just bore into this world. From violence and into violence, and yet the only person on her mind was her father and how she wished she could tell him how sorry she was.

Dad...

"Honey, is there someone we can call? You came in all on your own."

Dane wiped the tears away just as the doctor placed the last stitch. "No, there's no one."

The nurse settled the warm bundled baby into her arms even though Dane initially pulled back the slightest bit.

"Here you go, Mama."

The weight of the baby in her arms was as heavy as the weight in her heart.

The only way someone could hurt her again in this world, now that her father was gone, was through this tiny child. She made her vulnerable to every evil there was to man and Dane knew at that moment, she had a few things to take care of...and if it took her years, she would make sure this child was safe. Because it didn't matter how she was made. There was no time for grieving. The rape didn't matter now, but this child did matter, and Dane had to keep her safe.

SHE COULDN'T DITCH the phone. She wanted to. She wanted to leave them all behind, but she'd also learned that wasn't possible. She might need Nehale or Paul, as it seemed. There was no choice now. She wanted Matthew, but she couldn't risk him now, or any of the others. She turned the corner of the concrete building and peeked at him as he sat in the driver's side looking down. Of course, he had no idea what she was doing and if he suspected, she wouldn't get away with it. So she had to act fast because she knew it wouldn't be long before he realized she was gone. Ghosting was something she knew how to do well.

Slipping past the open doorway, she spotted Rebecca go in and turned at the last minute and walked out before she had a chance to talk to her. There was no way Dane was going to drag Rebecca and Owen through her life, not when she now knew they were expecting. They might be foolish enough to trust their lives to fate, but Dane wasn't. Not when there was a child involved.

The people roaming around the rest area were all rejects for one reason or another, many arguing with one another. Edgy. Distracted...which always worked in her favor.

It only took her a few minutes to spot the couple she wanted. They were hugging and sobbing and stood at a nearby picnic table. Her round belly leaned against the man told her it was a familiar scenario and they were exactly the ones she wanted.

"Honey, don't cry," she heard him say. "It's just a week or two until Texas figures out this mess. They're dealing with too much too soon. Go to your parents' house and wait. I have to get on the job. As soon as I can, I'll come and see you on the weekends. Walk me to the border and call me when you're home."

Dane slipped behind them and pulled the shiny keys from her bag.

Yes, it was wrong to do this to these people, but that never stopped her before. The poor woman was going to have to get a ride. They would find her car soon, though. She just needed to borrow it for a few minutes, until she could make a full circle and get in line again...in someone else's car this time.

Keys in hand, Dane flipped the fob around and walked the perimeter of the parking lot. Seeing that Matthew and the gang were still parked in front of the restrooms, she pressed the button and when she heard doors click, she tried it again to be sure, and opened the door, slipped behind the wheel, and pulled away without anyone noticing.

Taking a big breath, she looked in the rearview mirror as she pulled out of the parking lot, first checking the couple still holding on to one another by the picnic table and then glancing to the SUV where Lee just exited the bathroom and was headed back to the truck.

They hadn't noticed her absence and she needed to keep it that way for just a little bit longer.

And then she gripped the steering wheel. "Dammit." She slammed one hand into the side. Tears spilled down her cheeks. She looked back again and saw Matthew look up, look to the building doorway. "No," Dane said and wiped the snot away from her nose with the other hand.

"I have to do this," she said, and the tears kept rolling down.

42

MATTHEW

He already knew he'd find nothing even as the evil stares met his eyes. The *what the hell are you doing in the women's bathroom stare*, as he peeked under each stall. "Dane?" As if they'd never seen a man in the woman's bathroom before. "Dammit, Dane!" he said when he realized he'd come to the end of the row.

"I'm calling the authorities," a woman said, pulling out her cell phone.

Matthew grabbed the woman's phone and chucked it against the cinderblock wall, where it shattered into two pieces, on his way out the door.

"She split," he said when he got back into the truck. "We've gotta go. Anyone see her?"

"Not again," Owen said.

"Where'd she go?" Lee said.

"I...don't know," Matthew said, and he backed out of the space.

"Matthew, that woman's pointing at you," Rebecca said.

"Yeah, I know," Matthew said. "Owen, get the little man on

147

the screen. We've got some work to do. She's going to try to cross on her own while I'm busy evading arrest."

"She's really upset, Matthew. What did you do to her?"

"Smashed her phone," he said and looked in his mirror as the guard next to her eyed their license plate.

"Oh crap. You don't smash phones, Matthew," Rebecca said. "What's wrong with you?"

"Want me to load a domb?" Lee asked.

Matthew looked at him. "When did you become so devious?"

"Nah, just to distract them," Lee said.

Matthew nodded. "Is that what we're calling them?"

"Yeah, I'm thinking of patenting," Lee said.

"Nah, let's not hurt anyone," Matthew said.

"Just as a distraction. That guy's...oh look, he's getting into his car," Lee said.

"Release the dombs," Owen said with a raised fist.

"No," Matthew said. Then seeing the guard pull out of his spot with haste and turn on his lights he said, "Well maybe one dom-b. That's too hard to say. You'll have to think of something else to call them."

Lee watched out the window while he worked the control on the phone. "Yeah, I'll think on it."

As Matthew pulled out of the rest stop tires squealed as he took a look back and watched as a little black drone dropped from the sky onto the pavement in front of the coming police car and exploded on impact.

"Shoot, we don't even need a detonator," Owen said.

"Volatile fuel. If they hit hard enough, kaboom," Lee said.

43

DANE

The phone kept lighting up and beaming at her as she drove. Like a hot potato, Dane sat it in the seat next to her to cool off. She wasn't going to touch it in case she accidentally answered it. The one thing that bothered her, though, was the fact that she had nothing on her but the phone and her ID in her pocket.

There's more than one way into this damn place. Dane raced down an empty side road and through an older neighborhood. A little girl in only her underwear ran barefoot through the hot street and into the yard of the house opposite. In another world, Dane would have stopped to make sure the child was all right, but that wasn't going to happen. Not now. She was way past that.

Focus! Dane yelled to herself and searched each road she crossed for another way across the border.

The phone lit up next to her again. When were they going to stop? She needed to use the map. Checking all of her mirrors again, Dane didn't see anyone familiar coming her way. No Matthew in the SUV, and the Challenger was already on the other side. She was free. No one could track her...except the phone.

Dane pulled over to the side of the road, checking all of her mirrors again. She grabbed the blinking phone in her hand and swiped up, answered the call and barely heard a "D..." as she ended the call and pulled up the map. A burning sensation rose in her throat. *No, I have to do this now. I'm sorry.*

Widening the border of her current location, Dane inched through the map. She looked up at the road sign at the intersection, checked her rearview mirror again, then opened the door of the stolen car and laid the phone on the seat, where it slid down the back and began blinking again. The door slammed harder than she intended, and Dane put her hands in the pockets of her jacket and held her head down as she crossed the street of the neighborhood and headed to the farm field on the opposite side at a quick pace. She had a long way to go and the clock was ticking.

44

MATTHEW

This, he thought, *is what hell is all about.*

Matthew sat there staring at the empty car. "She's not here. The phone's here."

"Is there any sign of a struggle?" Nehale asked.

Matthew shook his head. "No. She took off."

Nehale tapped keys. "She probably walked over the border from there. She's likely already across."

Matthew started the truck and took a breath. "Get me to the next border crossing," he growled.

"Is she on foot?" Owen said. "Do you think she stole another car?"

Matthew didn't answer.

Nehale typed more and kept scanning another screen as Matthew looked around.

"Could she still be here? Maybe in one of the houses?" said Owen.

Matthew said, "No, Dane wouldn't go inside a house or endanger anyone else, if she could help it. Like Nehale said, she's probably already on the other side."

"Her backpack's still in here. She didn't have anything else on her but the phone when she left the truck. No water, nothing," Owen said.

"She kept her ID in a wallet in her pocket. She has that," Rebecca said.

"Nehale, tell me you tagged her with a tracker or something she doesn't know about," Matthew said.

"No, I'm afraid not yet."

"Okay, does Paul have any ideas?" Matthew said.

Nehale said, "No. He's on the other side scanning the border for her in case he gets lucky. It's a case of probability at this point. And in another ten minutes, if we don't find her, we will likely lose her."

Matthew drove north along the side street and said, "Yeah, dammit. She knows that."

"Okay," Nehale said. "I found a way forward. This might work."

"Nehale, this better work. We can't screw up now."

"Give him a break, man. It's not his fault," Owen said.

"It's somebody's fault. I just haven't decided who," Matthew said and checked the map for the next turn.

45

DANE

High-stepping through acres of dry feed corn left Dane's arms and neck hot, sweaty, and itchy, but the field provided her cover not only from her friends but also from herself. Those demons she kept on a leash were never far enough away.

"Get to her and then get the hell out," she whispered to herself.

The next thing she knew, someone else hiding in the field ran. A shotgun blast followed and then someone screamed in pain over and over again.

"I said, get outta my field." Then he racked the next shot.

Dane crouched on the ground, pistol in hand. *This is the last thing I need.*

But she wasn't the only one in the corn field. A few rows over, rustling started as someone else began running as well, and the second blast went off.

Dane shook her head.

"Get off my land," he yelled.

One palm rested against the earth. A drop of sweat fell from her nose, darkening a spot of ground below. The buzz of an insect began again in between fading yells from the farmer's latest victim.

Dane looked at her pistol and quietly pulled back the slide and palmed it shut again and nearly clicked it as it slid a little from the sweat in her hand. *Pistol versus shotgun,* she thought. Those odds weren't impossible, but she preferred the shotgun in this scenario.

"I know there's more of you," the farmer said. "I can smell ya."

Dane shook her head. *I can't wait here all day.*

Then Dane suddenly landed on her belly against the dry dirt when the sounds of several rounds from an automatic rifle went off. Her pistol, in her right hand when she flung her arms over her head, went flying.

Then silence.

She waited without moving an inch for several more minutes and through her eyes, she peered beneath her arm and through the base of the corn stalks. She watched for any movement. Then she noticed a single ant nearby and watched as he picked up a pebble, his antennae twitching. Unlike the other insects and birds, this creature kept up his daily rounds despite the chaos around him. Then he climbed up and over the hem of her shirt sleeve and marched up to her armpit. Dane tensed and suppressed a yelp.

She had to get out of there. She had to move. But if the old farmer was dead, the gunman was somewhere nearby, and she hadn't heard him move yet.

"Dane!"

That voice. She knew that voice. She lifted her head and the first thing she did was swipe her arm free of the ant. But he wasn't supposed to be here.

"Dane?" he yelled again.

"I'm here," she yelled back. "Why are *you* here? You're

supposed to be on the other side. I watched you cross the border," she said, standing up and dusting off the dirt and any other ants that might have found their way beneath her clothing.

"I can't see you, Dane. Can you come here?"

"I don't know where you are."

"Follow my voice, Dane."

She crossed over two rows, downing a few corn stalks as she went, the leaves cutting into her bare arms, leaving long crimson lines. She finally found a row where she could see the light at the end of the tunnel.

"Will you hurry?"

"I'm trying," she said.

"Just a little farther. I can see you rustling in the leaves. At least I hope that's you."

As she reached the clearing, she saw Paul standing next to an old blue pickup truck. The farmer was lying halfway off the back tailgate. A bloom of red soaked the front of his button-up plaid shirt. His shotgun was in Paul's arms now.

"You made it," he smiled. "Welcome to Texas."

46

MATTHEW

"Okay, dammit. We're in line again and no one, and I mean no one, in this truck is pregnant. Is that understood?" Matthew said.

"But what if..." Rebecca started to say.

"Lie!" he said, and Lee suppressed a laugh.

She whispered to Owen. "Why is it such a big deal in Texas?"

"It's an anchor baby thing," Owen said.

"They're going overboard if you ask me," Rebecca said.

Matthew cut a look at Lee and he shook his head as he held a laugh with one hand.

"Don't," Matthew said shaking his own head as he drove up to the booth again. The crossing guard didn't look at Matthew right away; instead he looked at the drones attached to the roof.

"Good evening, folks. What do we have here?" the officer said.

One look at the man's expression and Matthew's stomach sank. One man's anchor baby violation was another man's drone breach.

Moments later they were on the other side, finally.

"Did you have to let them have all of them?" Owen said.

"The dombs…" Lee said sadly.

Matthew shook his head. "They wouldn't let us through. It's not so bad. You can just make more when our fuel runs low."

Rebecca said, "They seemed pretty happy to take them off our hands. Boys and their toys."

"Okay, now we just need to find Dane," Matthew said, trying to redirect the conversation. He pulled over. "Lee, I need you to drive so I can yell at the little man in the box."

"Deal," Lee said, and they switched seats.

"We've got her," Nehale said. "Or rather, Paul has her."

"Is she all right? Can you get her on the phone? I have to yell at her. She broke her promise," Matthew gritted out.

Nehale had that kind smile on his face again and nodded. "She is unscathed and crossed the border through a field. They are currently en route to the target destination. I'm loading the map for you to join them."

"Good, because I'm going to kill her as soon as I get my hands on her," Matthew said.

"She doesn't know you've crossed the border yet. We're…" he hesitated, "…going rogue for the betterment of the mission. Paul and I discussed this scenario before. So it would be better if you kept your distance."

Matthew swallowed. "Are you sure that's wise?"

He didn't smile this time. Or do that kind nodding thing that he did. He just said, "I do."

"There's still a long way to go to get to Tivoli. Generally things are better off in Texas except that you're generally heading to the southern border now and there are infractions along that side as well, though for different reasons."

"What do you mean?" Matthew said.

"Along the northern border, people are trying to get in. But they've also closed the southern border to Mexico, and many are finding they're trapped on the Texas side."

"You mean they're trying to get out, back to Mexico?" Lee said.

"That's right," Nehale said.

"Oh, the irony," Owen said.

"What are they doing with them?" Rebecca said.

"They've become honorary Texans overnight," Nehale said.

"But they won't let them leave?" Rebecca said. "That's more like a hostage, right?"

"On the contrary. They've been issued citizenship and can pay the taxes they owe and then apply for a passport."

"Oh, so they can leave and then return? But what's to keep them from not coming back?" Rebecca asked.

"Yes, they can but now, they have to pay taxes just like everyone else. They got exactly what they wanted. Don't you see?" Nehale said.

"They have to pay their own way, just like the rest of us," Owen said.

"That's right," Nehale said.

"Can we get back to the issue we're dealing with here?" Matthew said.

"Yes," Nehale said. "But this is a valid discussion because as you can see, Texas is in a state of flux and things are changing rapidly. I'll monitor the situation and let you know if anything applies to our situation."

"What about our time clock? How are we there?" Matthew said. "We've still got a ways to go."

Nehale nodded. "Yes." He looked at a screen in front of him and nodded again. "They're releasing the database in thirty-six hours. The last injunction failed, I'm afraid. And...it seems the congressman who led that charge died this afternoon in a car accident." Nehale smacked his lips with a grim expression.

"They're not messing around, are they?" Lee said.

"Not in the least," Nehale said.

Matthew took a deep breath. Dane...if they only knew the trail she was on. And then a shiver ran up his spine.

"Nehale, keep us back but keep us close. Do you know what I mean?" Matthew said.

"Yes, I certainly do. I'll be in touch. Oh, and before I go, there's a delivery coming your way soon," Nehale said and cut the call.

Lee looked at the tank. "We just had a delivery. What's he talking about?"

Matthew shook his head. "I don't know." He was still mulling over their conversation and the consequences of everyone's actions. He wasn't going to push Dane. He wasn't going to demand to talk to her. He was only going to stay close as he could because he knew there would be a time when she needed him, and he would be there for her whether she liked it or not.

"What is that?" Lee said looking up at an angle through the windshield.

"Dombs," Rebecca squealed, and Matthew heard a clatter on the roof as they lightly landed.

"Nehale must have overridden the program and recalled them to our location," Lee said.

"I love Nehale," Rebecca said.

Lee said, "I love Nehale, too."

Matthew tore his eyes away from the map he'd been studying and cut them at Lee.

47

DANE

"Are we going to talk about anything?" Paul said. "Or should we just continue to drive in silence? Because we're going to be there soon, and we should talk about a plan."

She huffed out a long breath after a while. "I'm really fine with the silence, Paul. I appreciate you driving me all this way."

He laughed. "Is that really all you can say?"

She nodded.

"Dane, I told you how sor…"

"Don't. This isn't about anything other than what I'm doing in the next few minutes. The rest is gone. You've already explained and we're not going to rehash all the tragic events of my life over and over again. I'm getting her out of there. And then I'm hiding her."

He didn't say anything for a while and then she realized they were falling into an old, familiar pattern, one she recognized from decades past. They'd been friends. Great friends for many years. They'd spent time in silence, sitting side by side as kids doing their homework, eating meals, bored summertime fun on hot summer days, their breathing pattern long ago meshed into a familiar rhythm.

"And then what, Dane? That's what I need to know. What's the plan once you have her? It's a serious question. Her grandmother will hunt you down. It's a discussion we need to have."

She swallowed. She knew the possibility. "I can't think about that right now. I have to get my hands on her first."

"Dane, are you even going to recognize her? It's been three years."

"I'll know her when I see her."

"That's what I thought. Just so we don't make any mistakes, Dane. There're several children there. I have an instant test. If she's a close match to your DNA, we take her."

She looked at him. "I won't need a test. How did you know where I stashed her? How can you know, Paul?"

He took a minute and glanced at her as he drove on the long flat roads, going faster than any sign suggested. "I backtracked, Dane. I put it all together. There's a lot you can find on the Internet that will take you back in time. Zillow, public property records, and people who carelessly give changes of address through the postal service are asking for trouble. From there you can find any name or company and then find their mothers, brothers, or uncles on social media and voila, Bob's your uncle when you only thought he was your mailman. We're all connected and you're as findable as your coworker's teenage niece's girlfriend on Instagram. It's not hard, just unconventional."

"But I didn't leave her with just anyone. I ensured she was safe and well cared for so that I could come back and take care of the rest."

"Was that your plan all along? Take care of him so he couldn't get his hands on her and then what? Now you're dealing with the mother. Let's hope she doesn't have a crazy uncle."

"Does she?" Dane asked.

Paul laughed. "No, thank God. Just the crazy senator grandmother, I'm afraid."

"Don't call her that."

"Crazy?"

"Grandmother."

He nodded. "Yes, well..."

"The caretaker's off the grid. They're not supposed to have had the children scanned. That was part of the deal, but I...was told by messenger when I went back to Montana that their security had been breached. There was a yearly checkup with a substitute doctor and he ordered the customary blood tests when he saw they weren't in their files. There were apologies, but the damage was done. Her DNA is on that list. As is mine and everyone else's. That's what sent me into panic mode."

"Yes. I can see why."

He slowed the car down as they turned past a sign that read, *Entering Tivoli, Texas, Population 479.*

"Are they expecting you?"

"I don't know. You tell me."

"The answer is no. I didn't interfere. Not without knowing explicitly what you wanted to do about the...situation."

They rambled on in the low car on the rough backstreets, turning around one corner and then entering another long stretch of road that eventually curved at the base. "This place is so small, is it even a town?" Paul said.

"There's a Dairy Queen, so yes," Dane pointed out, though she had a hard time making small talk.

"Is that the unwritten definition?" Paul said as he pulled into a long white caliche driveway, tiny shells snapping into smaller pieces beneath the heavy tires. The yellow farmhouse at the end of the drive sat quiet. Paul turned off the engine and Dane didn't move.

He rolled down the windows and they heard the squeaking sound of an old metal chain as a light, humid breeze swung an empty swing on a nearby set.

"Doesn't look like anyone's here," Paul said.

"No, it doesn't."

She opened her door and he got out and followed her.

"You don't have to come with me."

He chuckled. "I'm not leaving you to do this on your own." He grabbed a case from the back seat and followed her up the steps of the old gray wood porch.

The screen door...she'd been here before, years ago.

She'd hesitated then too. Held the baby in her arms. The white quarter wagon wheels affixed in each corner of the screen. She knew the door well. It had haunted her dreams since the last time she'd been there.

She lifted her hand to open the door.

"Dane," Paul said.

She saw her hand shaking like a leaf too.

He reached around her and opened the door as it squeaked on the hinges. Then he readjusted the case in his hand to beneath his arm and gave three knocks on the old main door frame. On the third knock the door unlatched on its own and swung open a few inches.

He looked at Dane and she met his eyes.

"It's unlocked? Even out here that's not a good thing," he said and pulled a pistol from a harness at the back of his pants.

She did the same.

He nodded silently as she raised her hand and gently pushed the door the rest of the way open.

"No!"

48

MATTHEW

"Where are we going?" Lee said. "I can't just keep driving around while we wait to hear what's happening," he added, as they passed a tall, pale pink gulf-style Southern home with long white shutters hanging on one hinge as if they were bracing themselves for a long fall.

"Looks like a storm passed through here ten years ago and no one's cared to fix it up," Owen said.

"That's part of the appeal," Lee said. "It says, *stay out, we like things messed up.*"

"Pull into this parking lot," Matthew said.

"Oh please. Can we go in?" Rebecca said. "Tacos!"

"I am kind of sick of drinking clear liquid meals," Owen said.

Matthew nodded. "Me too. Go in and grab takeout."

Owen said, "What do you want?"

Matthew stared at him for a beat. "Tacos, stupid."

"Okay," he said, and Matthew watched as a few rough-looking people exited the restaurant but held the door open for Owen and Rebecca to enter.

"Not everyone is out to get us, Matthew," Lee said. "Probably two hardworking roughnecks out of work. Dane's rubbing off on you in a bad way."

"We can't be too careful."

"Yep, just what I said."

"Listen, I'm going to go inside and use the facilities while we have a chance. Stay here and get me if we hear anything."

Lee nodded as Matthew stepped out and walked into the old brick building. The concrete slab stairs were making an uneventful fall back to earth and were in bad need of slab-jacking. He pushed open the door and saw Owen and Rebecca standing in line. She leaned into his chest. They both looked up at him as he walked in and smiled. Owen tilted his head in the direction of the bathrooms and Matthew nodded.

He headed down the long, dark corridor and noticed the old speckled linoleum flooring probably had not been replaced since it was installed several decades ago. Brown stains met the faded and splintered wood paneling covering the walls. *Bathroom's going to be an adventure.*

Back in the truck, Matthew said, "Are we sure we should eat those? They smell amazing, but that building should be condemned."

"You not taking my tacos," Rebecca said from the back seat.

"It's always the worst looking places that have the best food," Owen said before taking a big bite of his own, juice dribbling down his hand.

"I wish that was a myth," Matthew said, eyeing his foil-wrapped meal sitting beside them. "Anyone have hand sanitizer? I don't trust the powered soap they had in there."

"Live dangerously, Matthew. You only live once," Rebecca said.

"That's what I'm afraid of," Matthew said and then said to Lee, "Any news?"

"Nah, man. No news is good news. Here's a wipe," Lee said, handing him a white moistened sheet.

"The tacos are really good," Lee said.

After he finished his meal, they watched people come and go from the restaurant. "Place sure is popular," Lee said.

"Are we sure everything's okay?" Rebecca asked.

Matthew was thinking the same thing. "It's taking too long, right?"

"Should we ask Nehale? I mean, they walk in, grab the child and then leave. That seems pretty simple. Right?"

Matthew gave an uncomfortable chuckle. "Yeah, that has wrong potential spelled all over it. We'll give it a few more minutes and then give Nehale a call for an update."

But that didn't happen. Nehale appeared on the screen right then. And he looked devastated.

49

DANE

Brown paper clung to her shin as she walked into the foyer of the old house. Her boot creaked loose floor panels as she carefully placed one foot in front of the other, her weapon out before her.

"Dane, wait," Paul said right behind her, but she didn't wait.

When she turned the corner into the living room, her mind flashed suddenly to that day when she handed her child over to a stranger. Pale sunshine poured through the tall living room windows. "Don't worry," the woman named Beverly said. "She'll have the best care, until you return." She'd sat on a green velvet couch, the kind that only a generation of careful investment could buy, an extravagance of the South. The smell of peaches hung in the air. Glasses of lemonade wept on a silver tray atop the coffee table. And it was gone. There was nothing there now, only paper and debris scattered across the barren room like tumbleweeds in a desert.

"Dane, stop."

"Where is she? Where is everything?" Dane spun around. "There's no one here."

"Dane, that doesn't mean anything bad. Don't run," Paul said as she bolted up the old stairway and ran down the hallway that held the nursery. And when she opened that door, it was as empty as the downstairs. She glanced in each room as she returned to Paul, who was on his phone standing in the middle of the empty room.

"Yes, pull all the records." He glanced at her. "I'll be in the car in a few minutes. Yeah, let me know if you find anything at all. We'll look outside for a few minutes, but you can get me here. Nehale, before you go, how's the other situation going? I know you're on the move. Do the best you can."

"Wh...at..." Dane began, but her voice was locked. Her heart felt like an anvil. And when she started to speak, she couldn't stop the flow of tears and could not keep the anger out of her voice. "What other situation?" she said, gritting her teeth.

"Dane, try to remain calm. Don't cry. We're checking things out."

"She could be anywhere!" Dane yelled. "She...could have her for all I know."

And then she couldn't help it. One wracking sob followed another, so hard she had to bend over, holding her hands on her knees.

"I've tried so hard to make this right. I've done everything I can do to keep her safe from that monster."

She felt Paul's hand on her shoulder. "You have, Dane. I know you've done everything. But listen. We're not done yet."

"What's that sound? Someone just pulled up."

"It's the others. I told them where to find us."

"They got through?"

"Yes."

Dane swallowed. She was angry but that all disappeared when she saw Matthew burst through the door and reach for her.

"We're going to find her," he said as he held her tight.

50

MATTHEW

There were cattle in the back of the property in an overgrown field just beside an old cemetery. He could see them from the back door of the place as he leaned against the frame. Their tails switched at the flies hovering around their backs. Or were those mosquitoes? Damn, the mosquitoes in this place were an enemy all their own.

"Let's take a walk," he said to Owen.

Owen nodded.

Dane nodded too as she sat near Paul, who was on the phone giving orders and had his laptop open on the floor.

"Don't go far," he said.

"Yes, father," Matthew said under his breath but nodded all the same.

Dane wasn't going anywhere, he knew. She was glued to whatever Paul would find out, but Matthew thought a quick walk within sight wouldn't do any harm. Something about the place intrigued him, knowing Dane had spent time here right after the loss of her father and so much more.

"I don't know how to say it," Owen began as they walked down the caliche road to the next property.

"Then don't."

"It's just us here, Matthew. What if Mathus got here first?"

Matthew shook his head. "The stuff in that house's been gone a lot longer than the last few hours. No, I don't buy it. That relocation didn't just happen. The furniture and everything else is gone, from the way Dane described it. There're no fresh marks in the drive. No dirt ruts in the ground. No one's been here for a long time. Months even. So I don't think this just happened."

"I hope you're right," Owen said, "but still, the mad bitch is coming and if she makes the connections, she'll come here. We should get going."

Matthew agreed. "Let's give the nerd man a few more minutes of searching and then we take Dane and at least get her away from this spot."

Owen shielded his eyes. "I don't know how the cows can stand this heat all day."

Matthew nearly chuckled as they walked into the old cemetery. "That's because these are Texas cows and you're a Montana man."

"No, I'm a Texan, remember?"

"When was the last time you were here?"

"A couple of decades."

"I guess it doesn't matter as long as you don't complain about the heat and the mosquitoes and the humidity," Matthew said, and then stopped in his tracks against the dry, brittle grass. "Man, some of these headstones are older than dirt. Samuel Barber 1752, Samuel Barber 1864, Robert McCann Barber 1958."

"Lot of…" Owen said.

"Matthew!" Rebecca yelled, and they turned and ran back to the house.

51

DANE

"What happened?" Matthew asked when he and Owen bolted through the door.

"Give me the keys," Dane said, her eyes menacing.

"Ah, no. Tell me what happened," he swallowed.

No one said a thing, but he was pretty sure Dane was about to shoot him or shoot someone else in the room.

Rebecca's arms were flung out. "It was Paul! He was talking with Nehale about something and then all of a sudden, he just got up and shot out the door without saying anything. He left his computer here and he took off in his car."

"Grab the computer, let's go," Matthew said and when they got in the SUV he got behind the wheel and handed the computer to Lee.

"Dane, get in the car," he said as she just stood there in front of the passenger side of the vehicle.

"Dane, I guarantee you, that woman is tracking you by now and we only have a little time left here. She'll find this place. You can't stay here. But let me help you puzzle this out. You trust Paul, right? Yeah, so do I. I think he's onto something that he can't involve you in, but you have to let him go. None of us, none of your friends have ever let you down, Dane, and we're not about to start now."

Dane took in a deep breath. She wiped away a tear and took one last look at the yellow farmhouse that she always imaged as a safe place for her child and nodded. She slid onto the seat and for the second time in her life drove away knowing there was a fight ahead of her. The fight of her life. Only this time, her child wasn't safe, and she had no idea where she might be.

"Get Nehale on the screen," Matthew said and Lee nodded.

Matthew checked the map and began driving.

"I don't want to leave the area until I know what's going on," Dane said.

"Okay," Matthew said. "We'll just find a place to hang out for a little while."

Lee said, "He's not answering."

"He always answers," Matthew said.

"Well, whatever it is, he's not answering now," Lee said.

"It's Paul. Something happened. They were talking about coordinates and then something happened, and he didn't say anything; he just left," Rebecca said.

Dane looked out the window at the low brush off in the distance and swallowed. When they got to the end of the road, instead of turning right, the way they came into the property, Matthew turned left.

"Where are we going?" Dane said. "I don't want to go too far from here in case someone shows up."

"We won't go far. There's an older neighborhood not far from here. Just down the road. We can at least pull in there and watch from there. We'll be less conspicuous with other vehicles around instead of standing out alone. Are you okay with that?"

She nodded.

He drove about a mile, and they passed a four-way stop and

then Matthew suddenly came to a halt in the middle of the road with fields on all four sides.

"What are we doing?" Dane asked.

His mouth became a straight line. He put his arm behind her seat and backed up the truck.

"Owen, what was that last name on the tombstones we saw back there behind the house?"

"The Samuels? Oh, last name—Barber. Why?"

Matthew looked right at her. "Dane what was Beverly's last name?"

"I...I don't know. It didn't work that way."

"Lee..."

"On it," Lee said and began typing computer keys very quickly.

Less than a minute later, "Beverly Barber, born in Tivoli, Texas, graduate of Tivoli High School, high school teacher, married a guy...Looks like this is the one, right? There isn't an address. Maybe that was scrubbed. Here's her high school picture. Is this her, Dane?"

Dane looked at the tall, thin woman with short blond hair. In the picture, she was a young beauty, one who aged well by the time she met her a few years ago. "Yes, that's her. Where is she now?"

"Well, I don't know but maybe we'll find more of her family down this road," Matthew said and pointed up at a street sign. "I mean, there's no one else around here. They might know something."

On one side it said Barber Road, on the other it said Shaw Road.

"Okay," she said.

He turned down the long road.

"Lee, have you had any luck reaching Nehale yet?" Dane asked.

"No. I don't know what's going on."

"Give me your phone, Matthew," Dane said, and she tried punching the buttons, but she couldn't get through either.

Dane shook her head. She just couldn't figure it out. What was he hiding? One minute, Paul was sitting there...

"Maybe he had the coordinates?" Dane said.

Matthew turned to her. "If he knew where the child was, he would not have left you and went for her himself. He'd never do that. It doesn't make sense."

"No, it doesn't," she said but it was niggling at her all the same when Matthew pulled up in front of a beige house with a long, low screened-in porch.

"Texans know how to deal with mosquitoes," Owen said.

Matthew stopped the truck. "Do you, uh, want me to walk up with you and ask questions? Or do you want to do it yourself?"

She'd already opened the door and stepped out without answering. Matthew met her at the stone steps and tried to keep up as she opened yet another screen door. This time they had to let it slap behind them as they continued a few feet to the main door and Dane knocked and then waited.

The door opened.

"Hi, Sugar," an elderly white-haired man said.

He had a toothpick sticking out of the side of his mouth and was chewing on it as if it were a permanent fixture. He held his hand out for her to shake. His skin, tanned by the Texas summer sun, made him look leathery but kind.

She grasped his hand and shook. It felt light and friendly.

"Hi. My name is Dane Talbot," she said, and he still had not let go of her hand.

He nodded and smiled with his eyes since his white mustache hid his lips. "That's right. I think I know you."

"Now, Dave. Invite those folks inside and don't let them stand out there in that heat."

Dane turned to Matthew as if to say, *Is this right?*

Mathew shrugged like, *Hell if I know.*

"Come on in," Dave said.

The woman inside had dark hair and pale skin. Her glasses reflected the light from the screen door. "Hi...my name is Jane Barber. What can we do for you?" she said.

Dane walked into the cool little house, a respite from the humid heat outdoors. "I...we...just have a few questions. My name is Dane Talbot, and this is Matthew, and we're looking for someone."

"Dane Talbot..." the woman repeated. "I think I know you," she smiled.

Dane had just heard that from the man and thought it was likely their Southern hospitality talking.

"Why don't you two sit at the table and we'll talk. I just made some lemonade."

"Give them a beer," Dave said. "Would you like a Miller?" he asked them on his way to a cooler.

"I don't need a beer, but the lemonade sounds good."

"Are you sure? Miller, it's the champagne of beers," the old man said with a jingle in his voice.

"I'll, ah...take a beer," Mathew said.

Dane looked at him.

"Being polite," he said under his breath.

"Have a seat," Jane said, and Dane pulled out an old wooden chair at an even older kitchen table in the adjoining kitchen. Jane poured glasses of lemonade for the two of them as Dane looked at the old house. It was clean and comfortable, with white-painted wood-paneled walls and lace curtains at the tall, thin living room windows.

Dane took a sip of her lemonade as Jane and Dave sat down in their chairs. She tried not to jump at the questioning right away since they were so nice and kind but when she couldn't take it any longer, she blurted out, "We're looking for a Beverly Barber. She lived just down the road by the old cemetery."

It was Dave who answered first. "Yeah, Bev. She's my cousin. She used to live down that way. Our family's been here since the beginning of time and before Texas even started. Boy, the stories I could tell you."

Good....good. Dane nodded. "Can you tell me where Beverly is now?"

"Dane, maybe you should wai..." Matthew said because a beat of silence after the question drug out at a snail's pace as the old man thought.

Then he blurted out all of a sudden, "Well, she ought to be..."

"She's out back, with the babies," Jane said, as old couples do when finishing one another's thoughts.

The legs of the wooden chair scraped the floor as Jane stood and said, "Come on. Grab your drinks. We'll step out and see them. I just thought you two looked as if you'd had enough heat, but we can go out back. The babies are running through the water hose to cool down before their naps."

Her heart could have beat through her chest at that very moment, as she willed her hand to wrap around the moistened glass. She stared at it first, telling herself to pick it up, but her arm would not move.

Matthew must have sensed her state and pulled her chair out for her as she stood.

It was suddenly as if she no longer had unconscious control over her own automatic motions, but instead had to will each breath, each step, as she followed Jane out the back door. Everything ran in slow motion.

Jane spoke, her hand grasped the door handle, she turned and smiled but Dane only wanted to get through that door. And then the light shone through. There was a blue pool of water on the green grass, the small kind used for tots in the heat of summer, and a yellow lawn chair, the kind that folded in thirds, and a head of white hair tufted out from behind the back.

"Bev? There's someone here to see you," Jane said.

Dane didn't see the children at first. She rounded the corner of the chair and the woman who reassured her once back then instantly smiled at her. "I remember you," Beverly said.

Dane turned again.

Her mind counted nine children, all running around. A dark-skinned boy with brown trunks on shooting the spray of a water hose at the others. A taller girl, skinny as a stick, with a pink floral one-piece, jumping in and out of the pool. A small black dog jumping between them all, and Dane's eyes landed on one child amongst the rest. Her hand rested on the dog's back, shielding him from the spray or wayward steps. She had dark wavy curls and turned to her with one finger in her mouth and that instant, Dane knew.

Sarah.

52

MATTHEW

Dane had her arms wrapped around a little girl and she was sobbing like he'd never seen before.

He didn't know what to do.

He smiled at the kind people who let them into their home.

"Dane," he said and patted her arm. "Maybe we should verify...use Paul's kit just to be sure."

"Oh, that's her daughter," the lady named Beverly said. "She knows her own daughter."

Matthew swallowed. "Oh, that's—that's good. Why, uh, did you move from the yellow house?" he asked Beverly.

The cheerful lady sat up in her seat. "Oh, I'm having the place renovated but then the builders pulled out because of the price of lumber these days..." Then she winked at him. "And I like to keep people guessin'. I just had a feelin' someone might be looking for one of my chickees after our little security lapse."

Matthew was about to ask another question but then he heard his name yelled from inside the house. It was Lee's voice.

"Who's that?" Dave said.

"It's our friend. I'll be right back. Just a second." Then he took a step back and told Dane, "Don't go anywhere. I mean it," It was a command, not a request.

Inside the darkened house, Lee's face was lit up by the computer screen he held in his hands. "I've got something to show you. Nehale said to play it for you guys and then to get back to him when you have questions."

"Oh. Okay. Should Dane see this too?"

Lee nodded. His eyes were huge.

"Okay, it's complicated back here but come on."

Outside, Dane held the little girl on her lap while she sat next to the old woman talking and the weirdest thing was, the little girl had her arms wrapped around Dane like a vise, as if she was never letting go.

"Dane, I hate to interrupt..."

Dane wiped away a tear and almost smiled. "It's okay. Something important?"

"I think so, yes."

Lee interrupted. "Uh, this isn't for prime viewing. Trust me."

"Oh, okay, that bad," Matthew said.

"Yeah," Lee said and again, widened his eyes, with a thin, straight mouth.

"Okay."

Dane stood with the little girl in her arms. It was the first time he got a good look at the little girl and he had no idea why he would ever doubt she wasn't Dane's own daughter. Same hair, but it was the dark stormy eyes that gave it away.

Despite all the danger they were currently in, he smiled. He wasn't sure the world could take two Dane Talbots. His heart melted right away when Sarah smiled up at him. "Hi there," he said. *Yep, big trouble,* he said to himself.

Then Lee said, "I don't think this is G-rated either." He shook his head.

"Well, I'm not going to be the one to tell her to put her daughter down. Are you going to do that?"

Lee shook his head but seemed reluctant to say anything to that.

Wise man.

Dane followed them back into the kitchen to the table they sat at before, though Dane held onto Sarah and turned her away so that she could not see the screen when Lee pressed play on the video they were about to watch.

Lee explained, "This was taken less than an hour ago."

"That's the house we were just at," Matthew said.

"Yeah, watch," Lee said.

The camera was fitted to the front of the Challenger because Paul had stepped out in front of the vehicle and turned to face the camera. He smiled and blew a kiss and then turned back and walked to a shiny black SUV parked in the driveway. A man leaning against the back pulled out a cigarette and began smoking as Paul confronted him.

"Is there sound on this thing?"

"No, it's just the video."

"They're arguing," Matthew said.

The man dropped his cigarette and grabbed Paul by the front of his shirt.

Paul grabbed his pistol from his back holster.

The back door opened and a woman stepped out.

"Uhhh," Dane gasped, and pulled the little girl closer to her chest.

"That's her, isn't it?" Matthew said.

Dane nodded.

"We've got to get out of here," Matthew said and began to move.

"No. No, we don't. Watch," Lee said.

It was at that moment dombs rained down onto the ground, detonating one after another like exploding marbles from the sky.

"Paul!" Dane said, closing her eyes and holding the little girl closer still.

53

DANE

Dane walked down the white caliche drive in front of the old yellow house. She smiled when Sarah opened and closed the wagon wheel screen door, slapping it against the wooden frame, a sound she would never tire from. "What are you doing?" she laughed as Sarah ran down the stairs in her bare feet, her brown hair wild. "You're still in your pajamas, silly."

"Matthew's making pancakes!" she said, with a crazy grin.

"Oh, did we find syrup?"

She shook her head. "He made some with apple butter?" Her brows furrowed.

"Oh, that's not right," Dane said and used her hands to try and finger comb her three-year-old's hair into something manageable.

Sarah slipped her hand inside Dane's as they walked back to the house. She could smell the bacon the closer they got.

"Owen said I could have peanut butter on mine. Is that okay...Mommy?"

It was still a strange sensation having her daughter in her physical life as she'd always remained in her soul each and every waking hour since her birth. Her heart lurched. It was the first time she'd called her the *m* word and it came out like a question, as if Sarah was trying on for size.

Dane squeezed her little hand in her own and even though the words were hard to speak she said, "Of course. Peanut butter's my favorite, too."

The TV was on when she'd left. They were celebrating the new drone food delivery initiative headed by Rebel Blaze. People celebrated in the streets of Chicago and the water improvement initiative was underway in the Rust Belt. Payment for protesting became illegal and punishable by large fines and jail time.

But it was the mere mention of Senator Mathus' untimely death earlier in the year that stalled the release of the DNA initiative and many other programs after corruption came to light afterward, that brought Dane outside for an early morning walk by herself.

"It's all over and we're finally safe because of you," she said, standing next to a freshly dug grave with a pile of dirt that had yet to settle down. Paul lay between two of the many Barbers who'd kept her secret safe while she was gone.

Less and less was Maria Mathus' name mentioned anymore, or others like her, who caused so much destruction. Their tentacles, laced through lives with a blade, were eventually severed and cut away like a cancer.

Still...it was a saying that was quoted by Gowdy that lingered on Dane's mind.

They were sitting there on the screen, across from one another as always. This time it was as if they both mourned for their side. They weren't enemies any longer, just both witness to tragedy. They'd both lost a war and it was like men do when they reanalyze what just happened. What were their triumphs, their failures—where did they go wrong?

"Do you know what bothers me?" Gowdy asked in a near-whisper, so that you had to lean into the television to hear him clearly as his voice cracked.

Cameron shook his head, his fingers held in a steeple before his face.

"This one quote keeps rolling through my mind now, after all the shit we just endured. A man once said, *Tomorrow is the most important thing in life. It comes to us at midnight very clean. It's perfect when it arrives, and it puts itself in our hands. It hopes we've learned something from yesterday.* Do you know who said that?" he asked Cameron Hughes.

Cameron shook his head again, as he leaned back in his seat. "I haven't heard that one, no."

"John Wayne."

ACKNOWLEDGMENTS

I am indebted to the year 2021. Without your response to the catastrophe of 2020, I don't know that the depth of pain Dane relayed would have been as aptly conveyed. Thank you to my editor, Dr. Vonda, who loved the closing of this series and remarked in comments often about her guesses. To my narrator for the series, Brian Callanan, thank you for taking on the project so perfectly. The series finally found the voices it deserved.

Additional debts are owed to my friends: Doug (the mover) who keeps holding out for my own story, (not going to happen.) The McCalpines, for putting up with me in my off time. John for his support during the loss of my father and the use of his image. Diana my work wife and constant support.

The largest thanks goes to Adam and Heidi, who are an enduring joy in my life, and to Henry and Hazel, who lace my evenings with purrs and humor.

ABOUT THE AUTHOR

A. R. Shaw is a *USA Today* Bestselling Author. She's published over 16 books and counting. She served in the United States Air Force Reserves as a Communications Radio Operator and began publishing her works in the fall of 2013 with her debut novel, *The China Pandemic* and continues the journey from her home in the Pacific Northwest alongside her loyal tabby cats, Henry and Hazel in a house full of books.

ALSO BY A. R. SHAW

Graham's Resolution

The China Pandemic

The Cascade Preppers

The Last Infidels

The Malefic Nation

The Bitter Earth

The Wild West

Surrender the Sun

Bishop's Honor

Sanctuary

Point of No Return

Dawn of Deception

Unbound

Undone

Unbeaten

Remember the Ruin

Rebel Blaze

Wayward State

Grand Gesture

The French Wardrobe

.

Made in the USA
Las Vegas, NV
04 July 2022

51093206R00114